Bloodthirsty

By

Flynn Meaney

poppy

LITTLE, BROWN AND COMPANY
New York   Boston

Poppy

Hachette Book Group
237 Park Avenue, New York, NY 10017
For more of your favorite series, visit our website at www.pickapoppy.com

Poppy is an imprint of Little, Brown and Company.
The Poppy name and logo are trademarks of Hachette Book Group, Inc.

First Edition: October 2010

Library of Congress Cataloging-in-Publication Data

Meaney, Flynn.
    Bloodthirsty / by Flynn Meaney. — 1st ed.
       p. cm.
    "Poppy."
    Summary: Awkward, sun-allergic sixteen-year-old Finbar Frame decides that his only chance to get a girlfriend is to pretend to be a vampire, while his athletic, popular, fraternal twin brother tries to encourage him to be more "normal."
    ISBN 978-0-316-10214-8
    [1. Self-acceptance—Fiction. 2. Individuality—Fiction. 3. Dating (Social customs)—Fiction. 4. Twins—Fiction. 5. Brothers—Fiction. 6. High schools—Fiction. 7. Schools—Fiction.] I. Title.
    PZ7.M5118Bl 2010
    [Fic]—dc22

                                                                      2010008620

10 9 8 7 6 5 4 3 2 1

RRD-C
Printed in the United States of America

For my parents,
and for all the books they read me,
far too many to name.

chapter

"Turn me," Jenny demanded, looking up at me, her eyes so intense they could have bored me into the brick wall behind me. "Turn me into a vampire."

Her neck was milky white, like a blank canvas or first-day-of-school looseleaf. The few freckles near her collarbone jumped out at me like targets. *Sink your teeth in*, they called. *Right here*. One vein in particular bulged, full to bursting. The jugular. Two years ago I'd been taught about the jugular vein, how it was the largest vein in the body, holding the most blood. My biology teacher hadn't predicted that the knowledge would grow dangerous in my hands. But it had in the past few months.

I had to admit—the opportunity was perfect. Jenny was a really little person, an entire foot shorter than me, ninety-eight pounds tops. She was not only a weak and easy victim, she was also a willing one.

The setting, too, was tailor-made, the stuff of low-budget horror movies and Mary Shelley novels. Jenny and I were in a dark alley. At her feet were dead leaves, litter, and a mangled pigeon. Aside from a brief flicker of light from three floors up, nothing and no one interrupted us. There were no witnesses.

But I was really, really wishing someone would come along. Lost tourists with Southern accents, pickpockets, whoever. I prayed for someone to interrupt us. I felt insane for having started this whole thing. This whole lie.

I've reached several points in my life at which, no matter what I did, I couldn't win. Here I was again. So, hoping for inspiration, praying for a miracle, I bared my teeth, tilted my head, and nose-dived for her neck...

Wait, hold on. I must be telling this the wrong way. That whole thing made me sound like one of those bad vampires, one of those horror-movie vampires who goes around sniffing out victims, isolating them, and draining them of their blood, turning them into vampires against their will. In reality, in that alleyway I was just as scared as Jenny was—even more unsure. I was actually hopeful that someone would wander in—a cop, a homeless man, a superhero. I was so unsure in that moment because I'd never turned anyone into a vampire before.

Actually, that's not true. I was the one who turned me into a vampire.

* * *

And, actually, I became a vampire under pretty normal circumstances. Not normal like the back-alley bared-neck incident, and not normal like the circumstances in fantasy books or horror films. My wrists weren't bound by bloody chains. I wasn't in a basement with the crosses and the windows covered. No one hovered dangerously by my bared throat. No thirsty fangs were at the ready. There were no splintered coffins, no Transylvanian castle, no rabid bats. No one wore a cape. Definitely not me.

I became a vampire in the third car of a train in Westchester County, New York. I was a Catholic schoolboy from the Midwest who was raised on Kool-Aid and overdue library books. And turning myself into a vampire like I did was normal for me, seeing as I'd taught myself how to tie a double Windsor knot, taught myself the lyrics to Tupac Shakur's "Changes" in Latin, and taught myself that if I wore a double Windsor knot or recited the Latin lyrics to Tupac Shakur's "Changes" in public, I would get beat up. Okay, those last two may have been taught to me by others, against my will. But becoming a vampire—I chose that.

Characters in books and movies rarely become vampires by choice. They're usually pinned against a coffin or a castle wall and sucked dry while they writhe in agonizing protest. Becoming a vampire *hurts*. Or, in my case, is a pain in the ass. To "turn" voluntarily, you'd have to be on the verge of death,

3

or so sick of the pathetic human being you are that you'd throw away your mortality for any kind of change. Looking back, I had definitely reached this brink, this point of desperation and self-disappointment. And now I'm trying to remember how I got there.

Maybe it started with the move to New York.

I grew up in Alexandria, Indiana. Well, I shouldn't say "grew up." I lived there until I was sixteen, after which I was hopefully still growing. I was already six-foot-one, but in terms of facial hair, I'm behind the curve, so perhaps I hadn't reached maturity. Anyway, Alexandria, Indiana. Its claim to fame is being home to the World's Largest Ball of Paint. What's a ball of paint, you ask? Fair question. It's actually a regular-size baseball with more than 21,500 coats of paint. You can check it out on our family Christmas cards from the past twelve years. We pose in front of it every year.

My dad was a regional sales manager for an electronics company. He was like one of those CIA guys who goes to the office and comes home and never speaks of what he does. The only part of his job he brought home was his love of gadgets. This really pisses off my mother, who's really nervous about things like technology and assumes that anything that plugs into a wall is a carcinogen. Although my dad is clueless, somewhere someone thought he was smart enough to be promoted to a consultant. That's how he got moved to the New York office. Apparently a consultant is someone who peers over your shoulder as you do *your* job and tells you how to do it better. I couldn't picture my dad doing this. My mother, on the other hand...

My brother, Luke, and I had just finished the tenth grade at this Catholic school, St. Luke's, a few towns over. Luke was a running back on the football team and a point guard on the basketball team. He had played both so well in his sophomore year that the coaches promised he would start as a junior. As for me, I'd been promoted to editor of the literary magazine. Okay, so I'd been promoted from sole contributor to editor. And, okay, the *St. Luke's Lit* only had a circulation of five (that would be me, the faculty adviser, my mother, and two anonymous students who had been too embarrassed to include their names in a survey). But "editor of the literary magazine" would look good on my college applications.

But I was pretty sick of St. Luke's. Despite my powerful position on the *Lit*, no one really respected me. Especially this kid Johnny Frackas, who was always bugging me. Since everyone called him "Johnny Freckles" (both for his own freckles and for his mother's full-body freckles, which were the subject of much speculation), he grew embittered and took his anger out on the closest person. Thanks to the school's obsession with alphabetical order, the closest person was me: Finbar Frame. Every homeroom through ninth grade, Johnny Frackas would hail my arrival in the classroom with "Good morning, Fagbar" and a bout of raucous laughter. In tenth

5

grade, I got upgraded to Admiral Fagbar. In reality, that should have made *him* a loser, because it was an allusion to *Return of the Jedi*, but somehow pointing this out didn't win me any points. And I should have been protected from this torture by my twin brother, who shared my last name and thus should have shared my homeroom. But Luke only showed up in homeroom three times a year, because his football and basketball coaches gave him passes to get him out of everything. I was left to fend for myself.

Monday mornings of sophomore year were the worst. Most guys were starting to get driver's licenses, girlfriends, and fake IDs that didn't make store owners laugh in their faces. Other guys now looked forward to the weekends, to house parties and playing beer pong and puking their guts out and kissing girls. (Hopefully not those last two simultaneously, although I've heard stories…) None of these things was happening for me, not even the puking.

It wasn't like I was never invited anywhere. In fact, my brother, Luke, invited me everywhere. Every Friday afternoon, he'd sprint down the long hallway that separated his room from my room and say, "Hey, Sean O'Connor's brother gave him three cases of beer. All the cans have dents in them, but he Googled it and said that we probably won't get botulism. Come drink with us!"

Or: "Maddy Keller's hot sister got back from Sweden and they're having a party. With *Swedish* girls. They're the hottest girls after Brazilian girls. Finn, you gotta come with. It's gonna be *uh-may-zing*."

Or: "Did you see the commercial for that horror movie where that Disney Channel girl shows her boobs? The team is going, come with!" Pause. "But there's *chain saws*, bro."

To my brother, Luke, a ball of energy and optimism, lots of things were *uh-may-zing*. That's because every time Luke walked into a room, there was applause and adoration. For Luke, every high school party was like a red-carpet movie premiere, and he was Vince Chase from *Entourage*. People were fighting to talk to him and ask him questions. Girls were tugging at his clothes and asking for his autograph. Guys were calling out to him with weird nicknames they'd come up with between Gatorade spits on the football field. Everyone was happy to see him.

I could only imagine how guys like…oh, say, Johnny Frackas, would react to me showing up at a party of Swiss girls and adding to the sausage fest. Or how Sean O'Connor would feel if a random nerd showed up to drink one of his precious cans of dented beer. Or how hard they would laugh if they ever saw me try to do a kegstand (Luke made me do a kegstand once when our parents were away, and I'd since been convinced you have to be a Romanian gymnast to perform one). It wasn't that I didn't like Swiss girls or horror movies. And it wasn't like I didn't like Luke. I liked Luke, but I didn't want to hang out with those other St. Luke's assholes.

I would never ever tell Luke that I was worried his friends would be mean to me. First of all, my brother never worried about social interactions, and he wouldn't understand. Second,

Luke took everything literally and might tell people, "Don't be mean to my brother." Which would, of course, have the opposite effect.

So sometimes I would give my brother a legitimate excuse, like, "I'm sick of hanging out with the guys from school."

Sometimes I would go a little more ridiculous and tell Luke very seriously, "Oh, I can't drink that beer. I'm really scared of botulism."

Or, about the movie: "I heard that Disney Channel girl is actually a transvestite."

Or, about the party: "Too bad all the girls in Sweden take vows of celibacy till they're twenty-five. No, I read it, the government makes them."

But Luke did not fear botulism, gender confusion, or the challenge of state-enforced abstinence. So off he went and I sat home while other guys racked up months of sexual experience. Every Monday, those guys would come to school looking all disheveled, like they were exhausted from rounding the bases. And every Monday, Johnny Frackas asked me, "Score any ass this weekend, Fagbar?"

Did I snap back with a clever response? Did I use my wit and mastery of words to craft the mother of all Your-Mom jokes? Did I take advantage of the fact that Johnny "Freckles" Frackas was such an easy target? No. Never. Never once. In fact, I never even answered him. I sat there like a wuss, shrugged my skinny wuss shoulders, or pretended to be really interested in my chemistry textbook all of a sudden. I never said a thing. And I really regret it.

So I was obviously glad to leave St. Luke's and move to New York. It was definitely an ideal time for a transformation — but New York itself didn't turn me into a vampire.

Maybe the whole transformation started in New York, with that girl on the train. She spotted me the second I got on and beelined for the seat next to mine. Although she was reading a thick paperback book, she was sneaking sideways glances at me every other paragraph. Her eyes took in the raised red patches on my hands and the bandages on my arms. Then she told me she knew what was wrong with me. And she seemed so certain, so understanding, that I agreed with her. Maybe that's when I decided my life needed to change.

Or maybe the need for transformation started fifteen years and nine months ago, with the fertilization of two very different eggs by two very different sperm. Sorry to bring up my parents' sex life, but that's how Luke and I started. My mother released one egg with her enthusiasm and energy, and another with her social anxieties and cheesy sentimentality. My dad released one sperm with his sports skills and his mild likability, and one with his tendency to hole up in his room for an entire weekend. The cool sperm found the cool egg and they hung out together in the cool part of the uterus. The wallflowers got together by default and made me.

The doctors told my mother she was expecting dizygotic twins, more commonly called fraternal twins. Two different sets of genes. Two different kids. One absorbed all of the nutrition and grew round and healthy. The other was mal-nourished but too sleepy to put up a fight. To this day, the first still has twenty-five pounds on the second.

One of us was named Luke, and one of us was named Finbar. It's hard to think that my lifelong bad luck wasn't confirmed by that name choice.

Luke was born into a world full of praise and admiration. And girls. My brother was exiled from the YMCA day camp playground eight times in one summer for being kissed by girls. It was actually unfair. My brother shouldn't have gotten in trouble; he was the victim. He was the one attacked by girls. He still is, to this day. He was the only sophomore guy at our school who was invited to a prom. This hot Asian girl from All Saints' Girls School asked him. And believe me, despite the school name, those girls were *not* all saints. My brother came home with his rented pants on backward.

The differences between us really kicked into gear when we were twelve. Luke came home from a boy-girl party with kids from our parish and announced to our parents that three girls had kissed him that night. Like, *kissed* him. On the mouth. My mother, who's a die-hard romantic but also a germaphobe, was torn between horror and curiosity. She solved this dilemma by asking my brother for all the gossipy details while driving him to the doctor for a mononucleosis test.

I also wanted to know more about these kisses (had one been from that girl with the rosary beads and halter top?), but by the time I asked, Luke was distracted by a fervent hunt for Fruit Roll-Ups. Where, you may ask, had I been when all this kissing was going on in the basement of little Mary's house? I was there. At the same party. But Luke had been in the basement, and I had been upstairs, watching Henry Kim play solitaire. P.S., the only thing more pathetic than playing solitaire at a party, even a seventh-grade party, is watching someone *else* play solitaire. Plus, I hadn't even known there was kissing going on in the basement. I always missed all the kissing.

Because telling my parents that I was hanging out alone with another guy while everyone else was kissing girls might have given them the wrong impression, I just shrugged when they asked, "What about you, Finbar?"

It's not that I'm not interested in girls. Just ask the priest who hears my confession every month. I'm *very* interested in girls. In fact, I'm interested in girls every morning for about six minutes in the shower. I have the sex drive of Bill Clinton. Even my obsessive love of books may stretch from my over-stimulated libido. Specifically, from the children's librarian at the Alexandria Library. This librarian had really big breasts. Actually, not big. *Enormous.* Each one was the size of an adult bowling ball. I swear. As a result, from my *Once Upon a Potty* days onward, I associated reading with all the things the female body represents: comfort, softness, sensuality, motherly bonding, nutrition, a sense of well-being...and *boobs.*

Because I don't get out much, in my mind, love and sex are all tangled up in books and movies. I've lived vicariously through Heathcliff, Romeo, Rhett Butler, George Clooney, Harrison Ford, and James Bond. From the safety of my bedroom, it's easy to believe I could be as gallant and brave as any of these old dudes. My mother, too, finds these things in books. Well, not sex. She's a stringent Catholic. But she loves love stories. Like a bloodhound, she sniffed out that romantic streak I tried to hide. I became her companion, her romantic-comedy buddy, her personal Oprah's Book Club. Let's just say I know more about the evolution of Katherine Heigl's hair color than any man should.

In many ways, the woman ruined me.

My mother's romantic comedies made me believe girls want guys who are thoughtful, dependable, and romantic. Sure, when the movie starts, the girl's dating the self-absorbed guy in the Maserati. But slowly she's drawn to the guy who remembers her favorite flower, picks her up from the costume party where she's the only one in a costume, and reassures her that her interesting mind makes her far more sexy than her sister, the *Playboy* model. The whole audience melts when this guy delivers the heartfelt speech of genuine reasons he loves her. His occasional awkwardness and fumbling only make him more dreamy. This is the guy I could be. This is the guy I *am*.

And yet? High school girls hate me.

Guys who get girls in high school honk their car horns and yell at girls with short skirts; they down tiny hotel bottles of vodka at school dances and work up their nerve as they work their hands up girls' dresses; they make fun of girls at football games for tucking their jeans into their boots and put girls' numbers into their phones as "Blonde" because they

12

never asked their names and never cared. Or because they genuinely forgot. That's how Luke is with girls. That's why he gets them—and actually, now that we're talking about girls, it started with one.

So that's where it started.

Celine.

chapter

But hold on. Before I launch into my tale of humiliation (the first of many), I'll tell you more about the move to New York.

In August, we moved from Indiana to Pelham, New York. Pelham was bordered by the beach and the Bronx, both of which Luke and I thought were awesome. Within a week, my mother had located all Catholic churches and emergency rooms within a fifteen-mile radius of our new house. Having grown up in Boston, my mother was glad to live near New York City and reacquaint herself with all her urban neuroses—about falling in that crack between the platform and the train, getting robbed in a back alley, being tempted to join a gang with a cool handshake, contracting diseases carried by homeless men and pigeons (my mother hadn't quite reached the level of sympathy that her oft-referenced role model, Jesus

Christ, had for the poor). She equipped Luke and me with medical masks and silver whistles. After deciding we looked like SARS patients heading for a gay club, we promptly "lost" both—in a very unfortunate incident involving the Long Island Sound and a receding tide.

My dad got a raise at his new job, so we got a new car for Luke and me. A silver Volvo. Luke and I spent July learning how to drive, and we both passed our driver's tests. I was actually a good driver. Luke was such a dangerous one that I think our evaluator passed him out of relief for having survived the test. One car for two eager teenage drivers—and for once, things worked out in my favor. I got the Volvo, sexy airbags and all, to drive to school. Luke would be taking the train to a Catholic school in the Bronx called Fordham Prep. Fordham had recruited him for the football team, and he would be taking the train every day. Fordham was a lot like St. Luke's—a small community, uniforms, heavy focus on sports, and all boys.

In a rare moment of true empathy, my mother had realized that I needed a change from St. Luke's School, or, perhaps, a change from Luke. She enrolled me in Pelham Public High School.

"You'll get to meet more people!" my mother said. "It made me sad that you didn't have more friends at St. Luke's."

"Mom," I groaned. "I had friends."

"Oh, yes, Henry Kim! I forgot about Henry Kim," she said. "What a nice boy. He was so good at math. And the violin."

(The worst part about my mom's shameless stereotyping

15

of Henry Kim, who was Korean American, was the fact that he *was* very good at math and the violin. Of course, he was also a star player on the varsity soccer team. But I didn't tell my mother that, because I didn't want her to know that Henry was better at sports than I was.)

This was my first time going to public school. This was my first time going to a different school than Luke. Most importantly, this was my first time at school with girls. But I had already met a girl in New York. Celine.

We had been talking online for four months. We'd met on an Internet message board called College Confidential. It isn't a dating site. Usually it's a place for high school students to post a list of extracurriculars the length of *War and Peace* and then ask, "Will I get into Duke?!?!?!?!?" Sometimes it's a place for parents to advise one another on which is a more admissions-friendly extracurricular, fencing or playing the oboe.

For Celine and me, it was a place to chat about colleges with comparative lit majors. Then our relationship got more intimate, moving over to Facebook and AOL Instant Messenger. We began talking weekly, and then every other day, discussing our favorite books and degrading their crappy movie adaptations. Once she went to a reading by Jeffrey McDaniel (a performance poet we both liked) and messaged me immediately when she got home. She wrote, "I was hoping you'd be on!!!" That was a spectacular moment. I could see my own doofy grin in the reflection on the screen.

Luckily I could play it very cool through a wireless connection. Celine had actually never seen my face, because my

Facebook profile had a picture of Tolstoy instead of a picture of me.

Celine was born in France but lived on the Upper West Side of Manhattan. She went to this snooty all-girls' school with the daughters of hotel magnates and faded rock stars and their second wives. Celine told me all these things about her life that she didn't tell anyone else, like how her classmates threw parties at their lofts when their parents were on Martha's Vineyard and got their malti-poo dogs drunk on Smirnoff Ice. Celine — like me — didn't drink, which probably made us the only two teenagers in the world who weren't chugging beer every Friday night. Celine smoked, but only clove cigarettes. Besides, it didn't really count because she was European. And she had tried pot twice, but the first time was only to see what it was like and the second time someone had tricked her into it with brownies, which she couldn't turn down because she had PMS (I didn't ask more questions about that story).

As a European, Celine surely appreciated someone with sophistication, intelligence, good manners, and a broad knowledge of literature and culture. These are the exact traits I've developed during my years reading in the Alexandria Library, smushed between the ginormous breasts of the children's librarian and Live Bait, the bar/strip club/fishing supply store next to the library.

Celine and I had upgraded to the intimacy of the text message after I moved to New York. We agreed to meet up in late August to hang out and get to know each other. We planned on a coffee date. But then I switched it up: instead of coffee shops, I searched online for French restaurants on the Upper West Side. I texted Celine: "Change of plans," and I sent her the address of the restaurant. She would think I'd found a great coffee shop halfway between my train station and her apartment, but *really*, I would wow her with a fancy dinner from her native land at a place called *Les Poissons*, which had good reviews of its food but also a review that declared, "The waiters were unforgivably rude." These two comments combined led me to believe it was an authentic French restaurant.

Yes, I know, I am a suave and romantic gentleman. In fact, this move showed me to have the elegance of Richard Gere in *Pretty Woman*, the spontaneity of George from *A Room with a View*, the boldness of Harrison Ford in *Star Wars*, and the technological skill of Tom Hanks in *You've Got Mail*.

But even when you've got a romantic plan in place and you're wearing a collared shirt, there's nothing more stressful than waiting for your Internet date to show up. First I started to question myself. From "Is there too much gel in my hair?" down to "Loafers? What was I thinking?"

Then, when she was sixteen minutes late, I began to worry about her. Was she still as cute as her pictures? Maybe she'd looked like that once, but she had gained three hundred pounds. Or had gotten her entire face pierced. She was now ninety percent metal and could never return to her home country because of the airport metal detectors. Or she could be an alien. Or she could be a murderer. Or she could be a man!

Seventeen minutes into my wait, anxiety switched to primal fear. I looked rapidly around the restaurant. Who was in this restaurant to protect me if Celine burst in with a chain saw and metal face? There were two tables of older couples, and by older, I mean old enough to order alcohol legally. Then there was a table of scientists in lab coats who were toasting to some discovery. Wow, that stereotype of the mad scientist wasn't so far off....

Until—

Oh. My. God. There she was.

I'd never understood what science classes taught you about matter, about the very physical stuff of existence, but there she was existing in real life, taking up a solid outline of space between the fancy glass doors. She wasn't text on my computer or a snapshot taken from above by her own hand. Celine was *real*.

And she was perfect, in a little pink dress that showed the golden-brown skin on her thighs and all up and down her arms, her chest. What a tan! This girl was a melanin goddess!

Improbably, she walked toward me.

The men in the restaurant turned to watch her. The *women* in the restaurant turned to watch her. The scientists turned to watch her. Then they all watched her walk over and hug... me. Yes, me, the slumped-over boy with the sweat under his arms and his legs jiggling. I could see the scientists furiously developing hypotheses to explain:

"What is *she* doing with *him*?"

19

I could sense them evaluating me.

"He seems to suffer from a lack of pigmentation," the oldest scientist would observe clinically.

"And from excessive perspiration," his younger colleague would add eagerly.

"He doesn't appear very fertile," the only female would surmise. "*I* wouldn't select him as a mate."

But the scientists could suck it, because Celine came up and hugged me! As her head pressed against my chest, her dark brown hair felt like ribbons. She smelled like she wore deodorant over every inch of her body. God. Wow.

"How great to meet you!" Celine said, pulling away. "And—the restaurant! This is... well, a surprise."

"Do you like it?" I asked, pulling out Celine's chair for her.

"It's certainly a surprise!" She laughed, folding her little pink skirt under her tan legs. "I thought we were just having coffee."

"I thought we could have dinner instead."

"Oh! Well, great!" Her voice was so high-pitched that I couldn't tell if she was excited or faking enthusiasm in a high-decibel range.

After I took my seat, we sat facing each other like chess opponents. I was looking at the napkin I was folding in my lap, but Celine was staring unapologetically at me.

It made me uncomfortable, seeing as I'm unusual-looking. Well, not *unusual* looking. I'm not a van Gogh or anything. But my dark hair is kind of shocking because my eyes are really light blue. Like, *really* light blue. Think Siberian husky. And, as I've told you, I don't have the greatest tan.

"You're very pale," Celine informed me.

I was startled by her saying that, just straight out.

"Oh, yeah," I fumbled. "Well…"

"I didn't know you'd be this pale."

"I described myself as looseleaf…" I began. We had exchanged physical descriptions via Facebook message. I had been honest, but focused on my height—my best attribute.

"I didn't understand the extent."

"…covered in Liquid Paper," I finished.

"Right. Well." Celine sipped her water. "This is a lovely place!"

For a lovely lady, I thought. Nope. Censored. Don't spout that weak shit, Finbar. You are already unworthy of her.

There was definitely a *Beauty and the Beast* situation happening here. Celine was even a French brunette who liked to read, like Belle. I could picture all these little bakers popping out of their houses singing "Bonjour" to her. Of course, I didn't have much on the Beast. He was über-manly and could kick some ass. Also, he was abnormally hairy. I'm not even *normally* hairy, judging from brief and frightening glimpses in the St. Luke's locker room…. Okay, I needed to stop thinking about body hair. And Disney movies. And how Celine was way beyond my league.

Man up, Finbar! Get in the zone! Keep your eye on the ball! Get your head in the game! Get your, get your, get your, get your head in the game…. No! Do not sing the songs from

High School Musical in your head! That is *another* damn Disney movie! Does Zac Efron have more body hair than me?

"So," I interrupted my own stream of insanity. "What are some places I should check out in Manhattan?"

Knowing my interests, or perhaps based on her own interests, Celine began to talk about bookstores. I was mesmerized by the movements of her mouth, picturing it on my mouth, so I didn't speak much. Luckily Celine was content to talk, giving me the poser quotient of every bookstore on the island. It wasn't until the waiter interrupted us that I realized I couldn't read the menu, which was written in French.

I gestured for Celine to order first, and she pursed her lips even more to order. God, French was a sexy language. You had to make kissing faces just to speak it! Celine ordered two different dishes. They sounded sexy but later turned out to be snails and exploded duck liver.

Was there anything written in English? Or anything I would actually eat? I scrambled frantically.

"Hamburger!" I declared in triumph. "I'll have the hamburger."

A curt nod from the waiter. He snatched the menu from my un-continental hands.

"Ahm—burr—gare," Celine pronounced.

Oh. Hamburger. In French.

"Om—birr—gahr," I tried.

Celine laughed lightly. As our food arrived, the conversation turned to Manhattan's coffee shops. "I just don't understand what Americans have done to coffee," Celine was saying.

I never drank coffee in my life, I thought as Celine compared the expansion of the Starbucks chain to "entrepreneurial genocide." *Maybe I should start.* Of course, to drink coffee, I would have to be a whole different person. A guy with not only body hair, but facial hair, too. A mustache. Maybe I *should* be a whole new person. If I was all sophisticated and disdainful like Celine, if I was all sophisticated and disdainful *with* Celine, I wouldn't care about everything so much. I wouldn't care about not being good at sports like Luke. And I wouldn't worry about guys like Johnny Frackas calling me a fag. If I spent the weekend drinking coffee out of tiny cups with a French girl and sported a mustache, no one could call me a fag.

Wait, maybe they still could. Scratch that. If I had a *girlfriend*, no one could call me a fag. So I needed to make moves. While Celine was chewing on foie gras, I spoke up. "I have something for you," I said.

Over her greasy-looking and expensive liver, Celine looked surprised. I removed a small package from my pocket and set it in front of her. It was a book with a ribbon wrapped around it, like a present without wrapping. I'd tied the ribbon myself.

"It's *No Exit,*" I told her. "I remembered you said it was your favorite play."

Celine looked at the cover as if it enshrined an object from an alien spaceship, something she didn't know how to touch or open.

"But it's not my birthday," Celine said.

23

"No," I said. "It's just a gift."

"For what?" Celine first looked confused, but then the confusion softened to sympathy when my eyes met hers. She didn't get why I was trying so hard. Disappointment and embarrassment swept over me. For the rest of dinner, Celine made an effort to be nice, like I was a speech-impaired kid assigned to her camp cabin. She smiled and nodded a lot, and even reached to touch my hand a few times. But she refused coffee after dinner, and the waiter delivered the check to me. I guess he knew I would pay because this was a date, even if it was the lamest date in the world. Or maybe he just couldn't fit a check anywhere among Celine's many plates, each of which had cost me…wow. My dad would really regret giving me this credit card. Celine grabbed her purse and I carried the book for her.

Out on the sidewalk, Celine abruptly stopped her diatribe against some kind of shoe called a FitFlop, and I said, "Let me walk you home."

"Oh…" Celine tried to glance at a watch, but she wasn't wearing one. Then she pointed vaguely in two different directions. "I'm going way uptown, so I'm taking the subway."

"I can walk you there," I said halfheartedly.

I knew the restaurant and the gift had been too much. But I really did want to be a gentleman to the end.

"Don't bother!" Celine's sharp nails waved me off. "You're completely in the other direction."

Actually, I had no idea which direction the train station was. This was my second trip to Manhattan ever. But I said,

"Okay…" and hesitated. Now it was time to say good-bye. Right here on this busy sidewalk. The whole street was lined with the tables of outdoor restaurants, so we were being interrupted by other people's conversations and lethal amounts of secondhand smoke. God, people in New York smoked a lot.

Celine reached up, popping onto the balls of her feet, to kiss me good-bye. No, not *kiss* me, kiss me. She went for the cheek. There was nothing romantic or sexual about it—even heterosexual Frenchmen kiss each other like that. To me, the kiss felt like a consolation prize.

The problem was that, at the same time, I leaned down to hug Celine. My head was headed for her right shoulder. Her lips were pursed toward my left cheek. As a result—

We kissed on the lips.

Or, more accurately, we collided.

The shock pushed Celine back on her heels. My arms hung empty in front of me like I was imitating a gorilla.

"Oh, Finbar!" Celine cooed with sympathy. She gave me these rapid little pats on the forearm. "I really think we should be good friends," Celine told me.

"Actually, that was an accident—" I began to explain.

"But nothing more than friends."

A falafel vendor had observed our whole little soap opera, and it was clear he thought I was coming on to Celine. Now he eyed me with suspicion and turned the long pointy sticks of his sizzling kebabs in a sinister fashion.

"Just friends," Celine repeated yet again.

Okay, okay! I didn't need her to translate "just friends" into French and sign language. So I said, "See you around," and walked away.

Was I going in the right direction? I had no freakin' idea. I didn't know New York City at all. So I removed my map from my pocket.

Uh-oh. Something else came out with the map. *No Exit* by Jean-Paul Sartre, the first English edition. Shit.

Looking back now, I should have dropped the damn book in the garbage. I should have just let it go. But at the time, I didn't want a souvenir of this awkward first (only) date.

So I doubled back.

"Celine!" I called from the end of the block. Celine was already crossing the busy street between two honking yellow cabs. She hadn't heard me.

A Frankenstein-like mob was clawing its business-casual-clad-way out of the subway station. These New Yorkers were moving at warp speed (hey, I lost the girl, I can dork out as much as I want). So I set off with a few jogging steps in Celine's direction. Seeing as my jog was slower than most people's walking, I hoped no one would notice my desperate efforts to catch up.

I called, "Celine! Hold up!"

But I'd lost sight of her. There were more people on that stretch of New York sidewalk between Celine and me than there were in the whole town of Alexandria. When the crowd parted, she was a full block and a half ahead of me. In order to catch up, I set off on a bizarre obstacle course. To the right of the hundred-year-old grocery woman. To the left of an imposing businessman. A sharp angle to avoid a double stroller; a leap over a pissed-off dachshund in a dog sweater. A sprint past a drag queen in size-fourteen heels.

Celine had crossed the street already. When I reached the curb, my chest was pounding and I was out of breath (and, clearly, out of shape). But my primal side emerged. I called "CELINE!" above a honking yellow cab, all Rocky Balboa.

Celine was enjoying a little French stroll by a park where the sun was setting. There were no lap dogs or transsexuals in her path—proving once again that life was unfair. Celine was ignoring the wind, which was blowing her skirt up around her legs in an attempt at a paparazzi shot. She also ignored me when I called her name. Maybe it was for the best. If she had turned around, she would have seen her pale and sweaty Internet lover sprinting at her—and probably would have freaked out.

But she didn't turn. I crossed the street but didn't have time to call Celine's name again. While I was looking ahead at her skirt, something hard tripped me up, and I lunged forward into a restaurant's basement cellar. My shoulder slammed down three cement steps, which hurt like hell, and I tumbled headfirst right into a box of peppers. I guess landing with my head in peppers was better than smacking my head on the cement floor of the basement while my arm was pinned under me, but they weren't even red peppers, which are ballsy and kind of cool. I landed in a bin of green peppers. Wuss peppers. How appropriate.

As I tried to push myself out of the bin, overwhelmed by

the smell, a large truck backed up onto the sidewalk in front of the restaurant cellar. Two men climbed out and began unloading wooden crates. They were bringing new food down. They wouldn't have even seen me if I hadn't tipped the bin over, spilling the green peppers everywhere, like boccie balls.

"Hey!" the first man called to the second. "There's a kid down here!"

"I'm just leaving," I mumbled to the two of them as I climbed the steps.

"Sure you're not tomorrow's white meat, kid?" the second man asked. They both burst out laughing.

Because people who mock me often do so with enthusiasm, he repeated the joke. Somehow, they found it even funnier the second time around.

I didn't even attempt a laugh. I stood up, looking as bruised as the green pepper that had been smushed between my ass and the lowest cement step. I brushed off my nice collared shirt, apologized, and left. And the copy of *No Exit*? I never wanted to see that shit again in my life. I left it buried beneath the peppers.

Empty-handed, I walked the eighteen blocks back to Grand Central Terminal. Neither those long city blocks of open air nor the bootleg Burberry cologne I bought outside the train station could get rid of my pepper stench. On the 8:43 train, a man in my car kept sniffing around my seat and mumbling to his friend, "I don't know why, but I suddenly feel like pizza."

chapter

I'd been rejected by a vicious Frenchwoman and sniffed out like an Italian sausage by hungry tourists. How could it get any worse?

"Finn! Is that you?"

This is how it could get worse. My mother. She would need a post-game wrap-up of the worst first date since Adam and Eve got caught trespassing. She emerged from the living room, where she'd been fighting with our new air filter. She'd bought it because our house in Pelham was older than our house in Alexandria and she was convinced it was lined in asbestos.

"Finbar!" She began fluttering around me like a humming-bird after a Starbucks Doubleshot. "How was your date?"

"Oh." I pulled the door shut behind me. "It was good."

"Did Celine like dinner? You smell like something delicious; it must have been good."

I smell like humiliation, I thought. As I took off my shoes, my mother followed me. I was accustomed to this. But, for once, she didn't whip out her brush and pan to sweep up the invisible but deadly molecules of dirt.

"Dinner?" I said. "Well, she ordered a lot of food."

My mother clapped her hands together rapturously. "That meant she liked it! And what about the book?"

"Uh…" I tried to avoid this question and escape her entirely by going up the stairs, whose banisters were now cloaked in toilet-seat covers. Look what happens when I leave this woman home alone on a Friday night.

My mother followed me shamelessly, up the stairs and into the first room, which Luke and I shared. We'd had separate rooms since the days we rocked out to Raffi songs, but here in Pelham, we shared a room. Luke was rarely here, between his football practices and all the friends he'd made in five freakin' days. But he left a stench of sweat and overenthusiasm to keep me company, as well as enough cleat-dirt to AstroTurf our bedroom.

Since we were sharing a room, it was a lot harder to avoid Luke than it was in the days when I could refuse his invitation to a Swedish dented-beer-can orgy (or whatever weird event he'd concocted). Nowadays when my mother found a warm bottle of Killian's Irish Red beer inside a loafer in our closet, I was there for her interrogation ("Finbar, is this yours?" "I don't drink beer." "Luke, is this yours?" "I think it came with the shoes. They're, like, Irish leather."); I was there when she placed the empty bottle on our dresser and filled it with fresh flowers and a little note she'd written about the dangers of alcohol poisoning. I was there when Luke frowned at the bottle and said, "Hey, I think I recognize that vase. Is that from Grandpa's house?" And when he spit his gum into the note about alcohol poisoning. But where was Luke when *I* needed him?

"Did she like the book?" my mother prodded.

I thought for a second. "It certainly caused a scene," I told her truthfully.

"Great!" My mother curled up on my bedspread and didn't even pick off the lint balls. She was in her element. She loved hearing about love.

"When are you going to see her again?" she asked eagerly.

"I'm not really sure."

"You didn't make another date?"

"Nah." I tried to sound casual. "I think we're better as friends."

When I turned around, my mother was giving me puppy dog eyes.

"Oh, Finbar," she said. "I'm so sorry...."

I was glad when my father interrupted. Popping his receding hairline in the door, he said, "Hey, Finn! You gotta come downstairs and check out the new TV. This high-def is really something. You can see the sweat on the—"

"Paul!" My mother was offended.

"What?"

My father looked a little scared. We were all scared of my mother.

"You didn't ask Finbar about his date!"

"Oh. Sorry," my father said. "Finn, how was your date?"

"Paul! Don't ask him about his date!" my mother interrupted. Then she scurried over to my father and lowered her voice, but not enough. "It didn't go well."

"Finbar," my father preached suddenly, putting his hands on his hips and taking up the whole doorway. "You will never understand women."

"Don't tell him that!" My mother swatted his shoulder. "You understand me."

"No I don't," my father said. "I just pissed you off!"

"Language, Paul."

"But anyway, I didn't mean *Finbar* won't understand women," my father explained. "I said 'you.' I meant a general 'you.' A collective 'you.' 'You,' as in, all the male—"

"Enough, Paul," my mother snapped.

"Well, Finn, come downstairs if —"

"Not with the TV again!" My mother spoke for me. "He doesn't want that kind of radiation—"

And my mother followed my father out of the room. Well, despite her best efforts, she'd actually made me feel a little bit better about losing Celine. Maybe I didn't need another crazy girl in my life.

My mother had a long-term plan to comfort me and rebuild my self-esteem. She hid notes in my laundry and in my pillowcase that complimented me. For example, the first note

I found pinned to my boxers told me: "Any girl would be lucky to have you." Other notes reassured me about my physique and, disturbingly, my sex appeal. Whoever taught my mother the phrase *stud muffin* should be prosecuted.

My mother's short-term plan was that on Saturday we would all get together for a family beach day. We would bask in the sun, swim, restore my sense of masculinity, and eat turkey sandwiches out of a cooler. The plan rapidly deflated. Luke bailed because he had a preseason Fordham football game that afternoon. He would be spending the morning at practice, leaving just Maud, Paul, and me.

My bedroom door swung open at 9 AM. Lifting myself on my sore right shoulder, I squinted across the room. Luke had already left. My mother appeared over me like a prison guard with orange juice.

"Wake up!" she said. "Beach day!"

When I finished the juice, my mother threw me in the car along with the collapsible umbrella, cooler of caffeine-free Diet Coke, and jug of SPF 89. On the way, my parents started arguing about my dad's new toy—the GPS in the car. When I hear them argue about mundane things like telephone poles and the validity of the expiration date on a package of raisins ("They were always wrinkled, Maud!" "Not this wrinkled, Paul. They're geriatric!"), I forget that they once fell in love. But they did. In fact, my mother claims it was love at first sight.

Picture it: Chesnut Hill, Massachussetts, 1978. My mother was a nerdy college freshman squinting through inch-thick lenses at the Boston College hockey game. She was giggling and pointing at the cute players with her two roommates. It was hard to determine attractiveness, my mother told me, considering the guys were in full masks, pads, jerseys, and gloves—and the girls had nosebleed seats. But somehow she fell in love with my father, a freshman scholarship left wing on the hockey team. Actually, she fell in love with the FRAME in white stick-on letters on the back of his jersey.

"I couldn't see his face," my mother would remember dreamily. "But I loved him. Right then. Through his mask and gloves and everything. Actually..."

(At this point she always looked around to see if my father was there.)

"Actually, to be honest, I thought he had about twenty pounds more muscle on him. The chest pads, you know."

So my mother was in love with my father after that first freshman year hockey game. My father didn't know my mother existed. In order to throw herself in his path, my mother became a sports reporter on the school newspaper. She thought they would develop a reporter-subject repartee that could build into love. My mother has kept copies of those college newspapers to this day; she interviewed my father for seven different articles freshman year. My father introduced himself anew each time because he never remembered they had met before.

Sophomore year my mother stepped up her efforts. She became a hockey team manager. At ninety-eight pounds, she lugged enormous duffel bags of skates and pads from Boston to Michigan, from Quebec to Toronto. She traveled with my father. She cleaned out his locker. She sat in a special front-row seat, right on the rink, to watch every game. There was an intimate BENGAY incident, the circumstances of which I've never been entirely clear about. My father was polite, always thanked my mother for the towels and Gatorade bottles she handed him—but never called her by name.

In my mother's sophomore yearbook, one of her friends wrote: "Mission for next year: MEET TALL PAUL." "Tall Paul" was written in letters all skinny and tall like my dad. This bit of pre-parental lust disturbs me, but it also explains my tendency to fall and stay in love from a stalkerish distance.

But my mother almost gave up her stalking—er, love. Junior year, she switched from the sports beat to the college newspaper's features section. She resigned as hockey team manager. She didn't even go to hockey games anymore. That is, until the Eagles made the playoffs. Then my mother went to one game, the first playoff game. She sat in the third row, just to the left of the glass divider. My father hit a slap shot into her face.

There was a frantic time-out. Everyone sitting around my mother stood up and swarmed her. My father clawed his way over the wall and through the stands, and through the people, with his giant clumsy hockey gloves. He stomped up the rubber steps in his skates, all the while shedding ice in the aisles.

"Everyone stepped aside, and I saw her there, crying, blood pouring out of her nose," my father says. This is how he tells the story. "And I loved her right then. I loved her. And I'd never seen the girl before in my life!"

* * *

The beach at Glen Island was a ten-minute drive from our house, and on the Long Island Sound, an inlet of the Atlantic Ocean. There weren't big waves or anything, but it was nice, with buoys and boats and the whole deal. After hauling my dad's ergonomic beach chair across fifty yards of sand, I was starting to sweat and really looking forward to going for a swim. I also wanted to get in the water and out of it before people my age arrived. My skin got pretty transparent when I was wet. I'd rather wear a white t-shirt than go shirtless, although I looked similar either way.

"Finbar, make sure you use the sunblock," my mom said.

"Dad has it."

My dad's just as pale as I am, but due to advancing age he's a few steps closer to carcinoma-ville. So I let him attack the SPF 89 first. I took his ergonomic lounge chair (wow, that was comfortable. Not really worth the haul across the sand, but…) and gazed out at the Long Island Sound, thinking all these deep thoughts about water and rebirth and losing my virginity. Or, rather, not losing my virginity. Not being within fifteen miles of losing my virginity. Not being in the same planetary revolution as…okay, you get it.

Suddenly a vision came to me. Me, all wet, a skintight suit. Sounds creepy, I know. But I was picturing myself surfing. Surfer! I could be a surfer! I liked the beach. And I didn't mind exercise. It was just team sports I hated. They're so aggressive, and I'm not an aggressive person. Not even at the dinner table. I always get the last chicken breast.

Two girls my age appeared on the beach and quickly confirmed my love of the surfing lifestyle. They were free of ergonomic lawn chairs; they were skipping along barefoot with towels. They were wearing bikinis that were as small as their sunglasses were large. That is, mind-blowingly small. It was unbelievable to me. That they could walk around like that. Their cupped butt cheeks exposed. Their tan thighs. Their round breasts. Yes, I definitely like surfing—or at least the uniforms. I could scout girls like this all day. I could be a beach bum. I could be a lady-killer. I could be...

"Red as a stoplight, Finbar!" my father observed over his blue oxide-covered nose. My mother came over. She was wearing a hat the size of the Rose Bowl. As you can tell, my parents are not embarrassing at all.

"Oh, no!" she gasped. She covered her eyes with both hands. "Oh, Finbar, I can't even look at you!"

Panicking, I looked down at my shoulder. I'd gotten a six-inch bruise in a rainbow of nasty colors from the green-pepper incident. But I was still wearing my shirt, so it wasn't the bruise that was freaking out my mom.

"How did he get sunburned that fast?" my father asked. "We've only been here twenty minutes."

"I don't want to look!" my mother shrieked. Then she peeked out from between her fingers and gasped again.

"Don't look at his face if it gets you upset," my dad said.

What was I, the Phantom of the Opera?

"What is it?" I asked. "My face is kinda itchy."

"And your arms," my dad said.

"They don't itch," I said.

"They will," he said ominously.

I looked down. Red spheres were erupting along my fore-arms, like planets with rings. I looked like a pepperoni pizza, only less delicious. In fact, not delicious at all. I was disgust-ing. There were some large red patches, an inch in diameter, and some that were clusters of bumps. And my father was right. They began to itch.

"Maybe something bit him," my mother said. "Maybe he got bitten by a New York bug!"

"A what?" My father was puzzled.

"He should definitely go to the doctor," my mom said, purposefully focusing her eyes on my father and looking away from my freakish self. "All right, Paul, you get the stuff. And I'll take Fin—"

She steeled herself to see me and then removed her hands from her eyes.

"AHHHH!" she screamed. My eardrums hurt. And my arms hurt too. And my face. And my legs, below the knee. I was breaking out everywhere, red and stinging and itchy.

"Mom, if you want me to go to the doctor, I'll go by myself," I said. "I'm not twelve years old."

"You can take the car, Finn," my dad said.

"He can't drive like that!" my mother said.

That didn't even make sense.

"I'll take the train," I said.

"Do you even know where the doctor's office is?" my mother asked.

"As a matter of fact, I do!" I exploded at her. "It's the place where you dragged me the other day to get eight vaccinations and a SARS mask!"

I tried to stomp off, but it's really hard to do that in flip-flops.

The doctor's verdict was: "You're allergic to the sun."

What? How was that possible? The sun is a natural thing. It's *good* for you. That's like being allergic to water, or air. Or something really important, like Pop-Tarts. I spent twenty minutes at the beach thus far this summer and I'm a monster? "Solar urticaria," the doctor continued. "That's what it's called. The sun made you break out in hives."

Well, I definitely wasn't going to be a surfer anymore. And I guess I wasn't going to school anymore either. Or church. Ooh, this would get me out of church! That was a good thing. But being locked up in my room like the Hunchback of Notre Dame? Not so good.

"Has the sun ever done this to you before?" he asked.

Of course it hadn't. I'm not exactly outdoorsy, but I'd been surviving summer afternoons outdoors since childhood. For every two hours I spent ogling the children's librarian, I would serve an hour at the Alexandria community pool working on my farmer's tan.

"Let's chalk it up to your change of environment," the

doctor said. "I hope it will be temporary. I would say avoid being in the sun for more than a half hour for the next few months. Okay?"

A half hour?

"I'll write you a prescription for an antihistamine in the meantime," he said. "And have the nurses come in to bandage you up. Gotta protect that skin!"

Afterward, I rode the train down to the Bronx to meet my parents at Luke's football game, all the while looking like an escapee from a leper colony. The doctor had given me a pill that cooled off my skin and I didn't feel as itchy anymore. But while I wasn't quite as red anymore (more like a peach than a tomato), the nurses had given me those wraparound sunglasses only considered stylish in nursing homes.

The nurses had also wrapped my forearms in bandages, from my wrists all the way up to the hems of my t-shirt sleeves, so from the neck down, I resembled the Invisible Man. But I was not invisible, even slouched in a corner seat by the train toilet. Toddlers kept toddling by and pointing me out. Stay-at-home moms gave me sad and sympathetic glances but pulled their children away from me in case I was contagious. A man in a suit assumed I was blind and threw two dollar bills into my lap. After this incident, I removed the sunglasses.

Hey, at least no one was sitting next to me. Until the Mount Vernon East stop, when a blond girl about my age got on the train. I hate blondes. I seriously do. It's not that I think blondes are too good for me. But *they* think they're too good for me. Every blonde I have ever met has dismissed me

40

immediately. From the *Playboy* blondes to the hipster blondes with short hair and glasses. Blondes always think you're trying to hit on them.

I didn't want to hit on this blond girl. I didn't want to look at her. I didn't want her anywhere near me. But she came down the row, passed three different empty seats, and then chose to sit next to me. She looked me over a little, which made me feel strange. I'm not usually the type of dude that girls cruise like an overpriced shoe.

At first, the blonde didn't say anything. As the train lurched south toward Fordham, she had her head buried in this enormous book. But she kept sneaking glances at the Ace bandages up and down my arms, the splotches of rash on the backs of my hands, the reflection of the oily ointment on my skin. The girl asked me, "What happened to your arms?"

Mind your own business.

"Too much sun," I grunted. Wow, being pissed off really made me into a caveman.

"I see!" the girl said. This chick was downright jolly, despite my bandages and rash. Apparently she took great pleasure in the pains and misfortunes of others.

Then she asked, "Have you read this book?"

I looked at her. She tilted the cover of the book toward me. There was a creepy stone dungeon on it, as well as bats and a man in a cape with claws and fangs. It was called *Nocturnal Terror*.

"*Nocturnal Terror?*" I said out loud. "No, I haven't read it."

41

And I don't feel like talking, I wanted to add. *Even about books.*

"Oh, it's amazing!" the blond girl gushed. Then she began telling me the whole story...all three hundred pages of it. She started with the ancestors of the main characters, and everything that had happened to them all their lives, and then the second generation, and everything that had happened to *those* characters, and their cousins, and their hairdresser's brother's neighbor's dogs...and so on, and so forth. I can tell you the background story of all these people (and pets) in six words: they all got killed by vampires.

"And so, the great-great-granddaughter thinks that she can change the vampire," the girl continued. She used so many hand gestures when she talked that I was scared she would smack me in the face.

"So she shows up at the castle at night. And there's this, like, attraction, there's this *chemistry* between them. Like a spark, you know? So they get closer and closer, and they *kiss.* They're kissing, and she thinks he has all these human emotions. But then he goes for her neck...and he BITES her! He sucks all the blood out of her body—"

"Hmmm," I cut her off moodily. "Yeah, that's interesting. Maybe you shouldn't tell me any more, though. You shouldn't spoil the ending for me."

"Right!" Blondie said enthusiastically. "*You* should definitely read it. I think *you'd* really like it."

I made a noncommittal noise and turned away to look out the window.

She only gave me one minute of silence. Then Blondie leaned in close to me and whispered in my ear.

She said, "I know what you are."

I jerked my head around and almost hit her in the face. "What?"

"I know what you are," Blondie repeated. To make herself clear, she gestured to my arms and my bandages. What? She knew I was allergic to the sun?

Then she pointed to my face, which was not covered in a rash. And to my creepy husky eyes. She knew what I was? What was I? She knew I was the loser in a genetic lottery? A future skin cancer patient?

"A *vampire*," she hissed.

Oh, Jesus. Blondes not only hate me, but they are *crazy*.

She pointed to the cover of her book. There was the vampire, a white old man with creepy fungus-looking fingernails and a face as wrinkled as an expired raisin. He was wearing a super-metrosexual cape. He had left the dead body of a woman in the corner of his creeptastic dungeon. He was chillin' with some flesh-colored bats who were probably his only friends.

How dare this girl? I am not old! I am not creepy! I am not a murderer! Most importantly, I would never wear a cape. Some kids I competed against in high school quiz bowl used to wear capes instead of varsity jackets, and they were complete weirdos. Furthermore, I don't sit around in some cold dungeon sucking blood and talking to bats, plotting to lure women down there. I have a brother and a family and a life! Okay, so I still have to plot to lure women. But I don't drink their blood!

Suddenly, the frustration of a week of accumulated insults caught up with me big time. I hated this blond stranger, hated her with a passion. I hated her blond hair. I hated her dumb creepy book. I hated the assumptions she made about other people based on their unusual medical conditions and their pale skin. I hated her dumb shoes and her dumb clothes. I hated her stupid necklace that said "best friends" on it and was shaped like half a heart. I hated whomever had the other half, because they were a dumbass for being this girl's friend.

"You know what?" I stormed at her, standing up violently (then falling into the seat in front of me because the train lurched. But I maintained my anger throughout). "If I'm so creepy, if I'm so *scary*, if I'm a *vampire*," I said pretty loudly, "then why did you sit next to me?"

"No," the girl interrupted. "You don't understand...."

"I do understand," I said. I squeezed past her, getting awkwardly stuck on her knees, but shoving my way through. Then I stood in the aisle of the train.

"I understand that you're obnoxious," I told her. "And that you could have sat next to that possibly homeless man."

The possibly homeless man across the aisle looked up at me.

"Or that guy who's awkwardly checking out that girl's boobs," I continued.

That guy, sitting in the third seat of the train car, quickly looked back to his *New York Times*, which was upside down. That girl, across the aisle from him, buttoned her jacket.

"But you didn't!" I told Blondie. "You sat next to me."

44

"You don't understand," the blond girl pleaded. "I really *like* vamp—"

"I'm leaving!" I told her. "This is my stop!"

I stood there, holding on to the pole, trying to not look back at the blond girl. Or at that guy who I'd called out for looking down that girl's shirt. Or at that businessman who was pissed that I wasn't blind—no way was I giving back those two dollars. And then I realized that storming out of the train was becoming kind of anticlimactic because there were about three minutes of agonizing silence left before the train finally stopped and the doors opened at Fordham.

chapter

I think my twin brother, Luke, is a superhero. He can sprint like a cheetah. He can do the hundred-yard dash in ten seconds. He can catch something, throw something, and swat at a fly all at the same time. He can do no-look passes to the shooting guards on the basketball court. Actually, he can pass to *himself* on the basketball court. He has the reflexes of a Marvel comic character and the speed of a hermaphrodite Olympian.

Our pediatrician thinks Luke has a hyperactivity disorder. Luke can't read more than one chapter of a book at a time. He can't finish standardized tests. He walked out on the PSAT last year and went to see an action movie instead. Then he walked out on the movie. Luke can't eat dinner without standing up and running around the table. He doesn't do great in school, and he makes some people impatient. During our childhood, three elementary school teachers, a zookeeper, and a museum guide at the World's Largest Ball of Paint all quit their jobs and not by coincidence. (My mother was sad when that zookeeper left the children's zoo. He was gonna give her advice he'd learned from raising baby baboons.)

In eighth grade, increasingly concerned about Luke's bad grades, my parents put Luke on a drug for ADHD. Three months into taking it, Luke collapsed midcourt during a CYO basketball game. I've never seen so many rosaries pulled out of so many purses so fast.

An ambulance rushed him to the hospital. The medicine had sped up his heartbeat, and there was so much blood rushing around his body that he got dizzy and passed out.

My mother has been neurotic about our health since she was knocking on her stomach and yelling "Are you dead in there?" at our nine-week-old fetal selves. So you can guess how much she freaked out about Luke and the ambulance. She never let him take that ADHD medicine again. In fact, she never let him take a Flintstones vitamin.

So how did she react when the weaker of her offspring arrived at the gate of Fordham Preparatory School wrapped in bandages?

"You look horrible!" my mother wailed.

"Hello to you, too," I told her.

"What's wrong with you?" my father asked eagerly.

I'm a pale and creepy virgin? Nope, not what he was asking.

"It's an allergic reaction," I reassured them. "It's temporary."

I was super thrilled when I saw that it was a pretty girl who was ripping the game tickets at the Fordham gate, seeing as I was wearing my best James Bond formalwear: my swim trunks, a t-shirt that showed off my man-nipples, and a Y2K supply of Ace bandages.

"Go Rams!" the ticket girl told me, making an admirable effort to focus on school spirit and not my arms.

She was a brunette, too. Brunettes are my favorite. Eff my lack of luck. Not only did I look like a freak, but when I sat down in the bleachers, I was one of the few kids with parents instead of friends. I was sandwiched between my dad, who was wearing a new Fordham Prep hat (my dad doesn't wear flat-brimmed hats because he's a rap star. He wears them in a very uncool way), and my mother, who kept accidentally smacking me in the face as she pointed to Luke on the field.

"Look, he's drinking water!" she'd say. "Look, he's lacing up his shoes! Look, he just spit! Oh, Luke"—my mother shook her head at her son from fifteen rows up—"that's not very polite."

My parents and I first spotted him with a cluster of other white-padded guys under a floodlight. Luke was playfully hopping from foot to foot. Other players were doing various homoerotic things that belong in the locker room: slapping each other's asses, giggling over secret handshakes, etc. One leaned over to slap Luke's ass, and my mother was proud.

"Look!" my mother said happily. "He already has friends."

As the announcer introduced the other team, Holy Cross, I ignored the field and looked around the bleachers instead.

How were there so many girls here? Fordham was an all-boys school. But girls were everywhere. There were girls in groups, leaning in toward one another to share secrets beneath wide eyes. There were girls in groups with boys, projecting their laughter into the face of the right boy, pitching their voices higher than the other girls, seeking attention. There were girls who really liked football, who climbed down the bleachers to sink their flip-flops into the mud by the fence and press themselves closer to the action. These girls were watching boys like my brother.

And Luke was something to watch. Fordham had decided on a running game that night. I think they wanted to show off their new Indiana running back. After all, the whole world revolves around Luke. When he was introduced at his new school, there were whistles and shouts like the *High School Musical* cast was on a mall tour.

Luke really was great, though. Dodging between defenders' shoulder pads, making sharp cuts and kicking up field dirt with his cleats, finding the open space and dashing into it just before it shut, letting the green-uniformed chests collapse into a pile behind him. I'd seen all of this before—Luke's dodging, darting, sprinting, and slipping-between. Luke had used these same tactics as a child to escape from my mother in crowded shopping malls and airports. You'd think my mother would have become Jerome Bettis trying to keep up with her son. Actually, she gave up most of the time. Then she'd send me after him. I'd usually find a sleeker route, along the wall, avoiding the people and obstacles I knew I couldn't hurdle or intimidate. I would catch up to Luke using speed alone, not skill. This lack of coordination explained how I'd ended up headfirst in a bin of peppers—and why only one of us was a football player.

In the first half, Luke completed three touchdowns. The other team, Holy Cross, was pretty good, though, and they were only a touchdown behind. Their defense geared up in the second half; they had two guys key in on Luke for most of the plays—a short-and-tall doofy pair who resembled Crabbe and Goyle from the Harry Potter movies. On the last play, though, Luke had a really showy run. He hurdled like a Kentucky Derby horse and won out in the end with pure chest-heaving speed. Then he did a victory dance that made me embarrassed to be his brother.

After the victory dance, Luke's teammates mobbed him and ripped off his helmet. They swallowed him up in a giant sloppy pile of man love. Somehow, by the time I had made it down the bleachers to congratulate him, that crowd of sloppy teammates had been replaced by a mob of girls. Jeez! Where had they all come from? He'd only been at this school four days! Further, this school didn't have any girls! But here they were, sporting plaid skirts of various uniform shades and sweatshirts that listed the entire roster of girls' schools in the area: Ursuline, Holy Child, Sacred Heart. My brother is magnetic north for Catholic schoolgirls.

And they were finding any excuse to touch Luke, even though he was so sweaty he looked like he'd survived a tidal wave. The fortunate girls who had arrived early were staking out the prime territory of Luke's bicep. Others used flimsier excuses: one girl's manicured nail traced the 5 on the front of his jersey; one authoritative hand rearranged his sweat-soaked hair. One girl even bent to tie his shoe.

Luke waved at me from inside his circle of girls.

"Brother!" he said. "Thanks for coming!"

"You slaughtered them, bro," I told him.

"And people said Holy Cross was good!" He laughed. "Piece of cake."

Girls began asking Luke questions mostly about his feats of strength and how much he worked out. It was a flirtatious little press conference. "How much can you bench-press? Could you bench-press me? Will you?"

One girl, a brunette, observant—much more my type than Luke's—looked me up and down and asked, "Are you a reporter for the school paper or something?"

I shook my head. "I'm Luke's brother," I said.

"Oh, his little brother?" She broke into a smile. "Awww."

She looked at me like someone who had the potential to be cute one day.

"Oh, uh, no," I said. "We're...twins."

Her pupils flashed from the bandages around my toothpick arms to my sunken-in chest and the goose bumps emerging on my legs beneath my swim trunks to my super-pale face and eyes.

Then this brunette said an obvious, truthful, and terrible thing.

She told me: "You two are nothing alike."

When I didn't leave the house for three days after the football game, my mother worried that I was antisocial. My mother has suspected me of antisocial behavior since last year when I didn't cry during *The Notebook*. After her prodding, I managed one tear. I didn't tell her that the tear came from the fact that I was home on a Friday night watching a Nicholas Sparks adaptation with my mother.

During the last few days of August, I used the excuse that the doctor had said it was too sunny for me to go outside. This also conveniently got me out of mowing the lawn. It also excused me from scoping out our seventeen-year-old neighbor, whose family was Italian and renting a house for the summer, and who Luke claimed sunbathed topless. I was so embittered by my recent experiences that I didn't want to see another teenage girl as long as I lived. I didn't even want to see another teenage girl's *boobs*. When it became early September, and also got rainy and overcast, though, I had no more excuses (neither did the topless girl, who buttoned up and went inside, much to Luke's dismay). To appease my mother, I decided to go to some museums in Manhattan. I looked forward to losing myself in mummies, dinosaurs, and other species who were past their self-conscious teenage years.

Unfortunately, my seat on the train was directly facing

three teenage girls. Didn't girls in New York ever go to school? Oh, wait, school hadn't started for me either. Well, I could just look out the window. Oh, wait. I didn't have a window seat. Oh, well. If I had to look ahead, I would focus on the books the girls were reading and not on the three pairs of crossed legs beneath them.

The first book cover had the typical Fabio-style romantic male lead. He had blond hair longer than the woman's and a piratelike shirt ripped open to reveal pectoral muscles that were bigger than hers, too. He was a guy who could speak five languages and perform award-winning sexual maneuvers. He was a seducer.

I could never be a guy like that.

On the second novel cover, the guy was swinging an ax dangerously close to the woman's face. She was still smiling. He was a clean-cut kind of guy, with a flannel shirt and bulging biceps, like the Brawny paper towel man. He could handle a canoe or a grizzly bear, and catch and grill a fish for dinner. Like that guy on the Discovery Channel who scoops the insides out of buffaloes and then sleeps inside them.

I could never be a guy like that.

The third book cover was different. First of all, the book was called *Bloodthirsty*, which didn't seem very romantic. The letters of the title were enormous and red and dripping with blood. On this cover, the girl was featured prominently. Although she was wearing a white lacy dress and making the sort of innocent face you see on kids in juice commercials, she had some pretty intense cleavage. The Grand Canyon of

53

cleavage. I admit that I leaned forward to examine this a little closer (hey, it's literature!), but then the *guy* on the cover caught my eye. No, not in that way. In fact, he wasn't sexy at all.

The *Bloodthirsty* cover guy was lurking in the distance behind the girl. He had bad posture. His arms were crossed. He was brooding. His skin was the color of paper. And his eyes... He had eyes like mine! They were spooky, crystal-ball blue. Why was the cleavage girl with him? What was this guy's secret?

The Brawny book girl looked over at the *Bloodthirsty* girl. She smiled and said, "I love that book."

The sexy pirate book girl looked up to see what the other two girls were talking about. "Oh, me too!" she chimed in. "How sexy is the guy in it?"

The girls all moaned in unison. Really sexy, urgent moans. Somewhere a sound guy for a porn movie was kicking himself that he missed it.

"He is SO sexy!" the *Bloodthirsty* girl emphasized.

But why? I thought. I was bursting to ask them out loud. If the guy they were talking about was the guy on the cover, what was sexy about him? He was thin! He was pale!

"He's so brooding," the first girl said.

Wait, *I* was brooding! In fact, I was brooding right now!

"He's so smart," the second girl said.

I'm smart! I'm smart! I can give my PSAT scores to prove it.

"He's so thoughtful," the third girl said.

Thoughtful? No one's more thoughtful than me! Hell, I'll

chase you down the street with the first edition of your favorite book!

What was happening here? Either brooding, smart, skinny, and pale had suddenly become sexy and karma was paying me back for the time my priest suggested I use self-tanner so I wouldn't blend in with my altar boy robe, or I had stumbled upon my own personal fan club. I'd dreamed of this day before. I would call them "Fanbars."

"I know," the first girl said. "I *love* vampires."

Wait, what was that? Excuse me? Pardon? Had I heard right over the conductor's announcement that "a crowded train is no excuse for an improper touch"? Had this girl said she... *loves vampires?*

"I started with *Bloodthirsty*," the second girl said. "After that, I read all the Twilight books. And once I finished them, I read *everything* about vampires. I'm obsessed with vampires!"

That was it! It all made sense now! Girls *loved* vampires! How had I forgotten about the Twilight craze? Robert Pattinson and his pale mug everywhere? His accepting Hottest Dude awards or Best Kisser awards or whatever awards Nickelodeon and MTV thought up?

So that meant that the blond girl from the train car hadn't been insulting me by calling me a vampire. She hadn't thought I was a bloodsucking killer. She had thought I was a bloodsucking killer with *sex appeal.*

And she hadn't sat next to me because she was deranged. She wasn't deranged. She was attracted to me! Okay, some might think those are the same thing.

Optimism and a sense of power flooded me, a sense of power that's pretty unusual when you're six-foot-one and weigh only 130 pounds. Maybe I couldn't be a Brawny paper towel man or a bodice-ripping foreign lover. Frankly, I couldn't even unhook a bra. But when it came to being pale and dead-looking, when it came to being old-fashioned and a little bit strange, I could ride this trend like no one else.

I would become a vampire.

When a storm broke over the electrical lines of the train, it seemed the perfect time to christen myself. The early fall heat sparked into a sharp sliver of lightning, small through the train window, and I became a new man. A brave, fearless, fearsome man. A bloodthirsty man.

I stood up and (silently) declared myself: Finbar Frame, vampire.

Then the train conductor walked through and told me to sit down. He also gave me a suspicious look, like I'd been inappropriately touching people. I think he sensed my newfound power and was threatened by it.

But I did sit down.

chapter

With only seventy-two hours left before school started, I was off to a magical place that would be the source of all my vampire secrets and power. The Pelham Public Library. I still believed books could change your life, even though they hadn't worked during my previous attempted transformations (see the still shrink-wrapped copy of *Weightlifting for Wimps* on the third level of my bookshelf).

Thank God for my kick-ass attention span. Between Saturday and Tuesday morning, I read the following books: "The Family of the Vourdalak," by Count Alexis Tolstoy; *Carmilla*, by Joseph Sheridan Le Fanu (this one had some really cool lesbian vibes going on like 150 years before Marissa kissed Alex on *The OC*); *Dracula*, by Bram Stoker (this one I just flipped through; I've read it twice before. I also saw it acted out in the episode of *Degrassi* where Emma gets gonorrhea);

Revelations in Black, by Carl Jacobi; *'Salem's Lot* and "The Night Flier," by Stephen King; *Carpe Jugulum*, by Terry Pratchett; four books by Anne Rice; two House of Night books by P. C. and Kristin Cast; and Stephenie Meyer's Twilight Saga.

Getting any reading done, much less this many books in one nerdy weekend, was an impressive feat considering I shared a room with Luke. In Alexandria, we'd had rooms at opposite ends of a hallway, and I'd only heard about his cracking a wooden ceiling beam with a basketball, his using his bed as a trampoline and swinging from the window sash. In Pelham, I got to experience it firsthand.

At some point in my research, when I already had, like, twelve paper cuts, I heard Luke pounding his way up the stairs. The lamps in our room were trembling in fear of him. I swear, the kid's a portable earthquake. I looked around quickly. All the book covers on my bed looked suspicious and creepy—knives, blood, some bare female chests. So I scooped up five of them and shoved them into the crack between my bed and the wall, where I kept all my other suspicious and creepy stuff like my Megan Fox *Transformers* poster (it's life-size, and you can totally see one of her nipples).

Luke banged open the door, his white headphones blaring and his shirt soaked through with sweat. He lifted it over his head while he walked to his bed. My brother walks around shirtless more than Mario Lopez.

"Summer reading?" Luke's pecs asked me.

Yeah, right. I'd completed the Pelham summer reading

list by the fourth of July. Summer reading is my favorite thing in the world!

"Just reading," I said.

"Hey, when are we going to the beach again?" Luke asked. "I never got to go."

"The beach made my skin boil," I told him.

Luke shrugged. "Mom said she enjoyed it."

I rolled my eyes. Then I put *The Queen of the Damned* down on my bedspread. Although I never thought I'd say this, I was sick of reading. I decided to do what the rest of the country did instead of reading: watch TV.

"Hey," I asked Luke, "did you ever watch *True Blood*?"

Luke took one of the towels we shared and rubbed it over his head, neck, and chest. Reminder: never use that towel again.

"What's that?" he asked.

"A show on HBO," I said. "There's vampires."

"What happens on it?" Luke pulled a polo shirt over his head.

Retaining Luke's attention requires a team of Mexican soap opera scriptwriters, but he agreed to watch the DVDs and followed me downstairs to the den, where we have that enormous HD television whose radiation my mother fears. I put the first season in the DVD player and got absorbed in the show almost immediately. My brother, ADHD poster child, left the room whenever no one was being killed or having really noisy sex. Luckily, there were a lot of murders and a hell of a lot of sex (maybe becoming a vampire would be more fun than I predicted). Luke was better able to pay attention when he watched while simultaneously trying to balance on this wooden board on wheels. That balance board is the first physical manifestation of my father's midlife crisis. He bought it to work on his balance when he decided to become a surfer. That never worked out for him. Or me. Apparently delusions of surfdom run in our family.

While Luke balanced (or, rather, crashed into the couch, like, three times), I let all the information I'd read and watched come together. Every book had a different take on how vampires worked. For example—how were vampires made? Bram Stoker, who wrote *Dracula*, said it took three bites from a vampire to "turn" a human. The House of Night books said that becoming a vampire was an automatic physical change, like puberty (and God knows, I didn't want to relive puberty. I think I would have rather turned into a vampire than get braces with red rubber bands). And what was the deal with vampires and the sun? In *True Blood*, sun shriveled up vampires until they dropped dead. In the Twilight books, sun doesn't hurt vampires but reveals their super-beautiful skin. Well, I didn't have to worry about that.

But there were a lot of "vampire rules" I couldn't possibly follow. For example, True Blood is actually the name for this fake blood drink that Bill Compton and the other HBO vampires drink instead of biting people, which reminded me: vampires can't eat. This led me to realize that vampires also can't drink, or breathe. Eating, drinking, and breathing? I probably couldn't kick those little habits. Also, according to my books, vampires freak out if they see religious symbols, like crosses or Christian statues. If this were the case for me, I wouldn't be able to enter my own home. My mom has saints and Virgin Marys camping out all over our backyard.

But I realized, as I watched the on-screen vampires with their deep, drawling voices, their slick movements, their secret-agent reflexes, and the way they drew the attention of everybody (mostly every girl) when they walked into a bar or a party, that there was more to the vampire image than drinking blood and biting people. There was even more to vampires than those things I was good at—the brooding, the solitude, the old-fashioned determination to act like a gentleman with girls, the intelligence and knowledge of history. There was something more than that: vampire *attitude*.

Maybe I didn't have vampire attitude down yet because there was one important vampire book I had yet to read. The book that had started it all. That bible of vampiric seduction: *Bloodthirsty*. To be honest, I was too embarrassed to buy the book, even online. *Bloodthirsty* was a romance novel. Ninety percent of its readers were female. If I ordered it online, I'd probably get on some sappy romance novel list and get e-mails with pictures of shirtless men with long blond hair.

But if I was using this vampire thing to get girls, I had to read *Bloodthirsty*. So I sucked it up and went back to the library. I strolled the romance novel aisle between two twelve-year-old girls who were giggling and asking each other, "What's a member? Like a member of a club?" I managed to stealthily slip *Bloodthirsty* off the shelf. There had been seven copies of the book, and five of them had already been taken out—a good sign about the continued popularity of vampires. Concealing my *Bloodthirsty* between two more macho Stephen King novels, I casually strolled to check them out.

Agnes, a librarian who already knew me by name, smiled as she took my card. But when she saw *Bloodthirsty*, she shook her head.

"You can't have this one," Agnes said.

What? She was taking this mother—or grandmother—role too far.

"There's a parental warning on this book," Agnes told me.

"Books can have that?" I asked.

I thought parental warnings were for video games where you could steal cars and pick up anime prostitutes.

"I can call your mother and get permission over the phone," Agnes suggested.

I looked down at the cover of *Bloodthirsty*, with the young woman's breasts featured prominently.

"No thanks."

When I first settled down in a dark, private corner of the Pelham Public Library to read *Bloodthirsty* without checking it out, I didn't see why the book was so forbidden. The first chapter was poorly written, but not very scandalous. The story started off as a harmless *Dracula* rip-off with a bunch of cheesy dialogue. This English girl, Virginia White, is chosen to deliver a message to this rugged mountain town in Eastern Europe, despite the fact that she is a terrible messenger, can't climb mountains, and wears white dresses everywhere, which is dumb to do in a rural place. Anyway, Virginia White ends up at the estate of Chauncey Castle, who used to be a professor at Oxford but did some controversial research into immortality and drinking blood and got kicked out. Now, everyone's saying he's a vampire, but dumb Virginia wanders into his estate anyway.

For forty days and nights, she had been a prisoner of his home, her lily-white wrists bound by heavy metal chains....But now, unchained, she had become a prisoner of Chauncey's mysterious allure, and a prisoner of her own lust. Everything about him set her girlish heart pounding. His alabaster skin.

(Attractive, of course.)

His extensive vocabulary.

(A very sexy attribute.)

And his ironic struggle to find the right words with her, in their stolen, conflicted moments of passion.

(That's right, give the guy a break. Not even vampires understand women!)

The gay suitors of her girlhood, with their red ascots and horse races, seemed shallow compared with Chauncey.

(Hell, yeah! Ditch those jocks!)

If the rumors were true, Chauncey Castle hadn't left the Chateau Sangre in eighty years. Yet he was, more than any man she had known, an explorer of worlds: the worlds in his leather-bound books — Perhaps an explorer of her worlds, the undiscovered worlds beneath her silk skirt, her petticoat, the satin laces of her corset...

She pressed herself against him, with nothing between them but her young, ample bosom, quivering bare and exposed like two pheasants trembling before a hunter. Chauncey's chest, when she raised her hand to it, was cold and hard — as cold, hard, and unyielding as his own castle walls.

"I cannot feel a heartbeat," Virginia told him, breathless. "Do you even have a heart?"

"What does it matter what I do or do not have?" Chauncey asked, averting his eyes. When they returned their gaze to Virginia, they pierced her like swords of pleasure. It was as if the two were in a lustful duel and he had the upper hand....

"All that matters is what I am."

"What are you?"

"I cannot tell you what I am."

(Wow, this guy is some smooth talker.)

Luckily Chauncey didn't talk much longer. Virginia White took over the dialogue, and jeez did she have a filthy mouth for a maid from Sheepfordshire.

"Now I know where all that blood you drink goes," she said, rubbing his engorged...

"Oh em gee." The two girls from the romance novel section were giggling above me.

Feeling a heavy embarrassed flush, I looked up at them. They were both raising eyebrows at the page I was reading.

"Member," one whispered meaningfully.

I scrambled quickly to my feet and closed the book, saying, "Uh, this isn't the fitness section?"

After reading most of *Bloodthirsty*, I had learned eight new metaphors for erections, but hadn't learned much about vampire attitude. I guess I needed to immerse myself in the lifestyle in order to understand the attitude. So for the rest of Labor Day weekend, I practiced vampiric habits around my family to test their reaction.

I began by reducing the amount of food I ate in public. I didn't plan on starving myself to prove I was a vampire, but I also didn't want to be seen winning a hot dog eating contest or anything. So when my dad grilled me a mouthwatering pound-and-a-half burger on his new grill, I turned it down.

"Just the way you like it, Finbar," my dad announced, flipping the burger onto the toasted bun waiting on a paper plate. The paper plate was almost immediately soaked in beef juices. "No lettuce, no tomato, no ketchup, no mustard, no barbecue sauce."

I'm a very plain eater. In addition to my sensitive soul and sensitive skin, I have sensitive taste buds. So this burger was my Holy Grail. My stomach growled and I even drooled a little bit.

But I said, "Uh, no thanks. I think I'll just have something later."

What a terrible weekend for my father to buy a grill the size of Peyton Manning.

I adopted a vampire lifestyle as I lounged around the house, isolating myself from others, reading a lot of books, and glowering at my mother when she ran over my foot with the Swiffer mop. Curiously, no one seemed to notice me acting any differently.

Well, clearly I needed to step up the attitude. And I knew exactly how—with a deadly stare. Legends, movies, and X-rated books say a vampire's stare is so powerful that by merely looking a mortal in the eyes he can bend that person to his will. I tested this theory on my brother. Don't worry, he wasn't hurt.

Every morning of the summer Luke would leave for a run at seven AM. He'd return at eight, pounding up the staircase like a full corps of Marines, knocking the door open with a sweaty arm and ruining my REM sleep with the latest pop song blaring out of his iPod headphones. Lacking my discriminating taste in music, Luke always downloaded whatever was playing incessantly on the radio. On this Labor Day Monday, the last day of summer vacation, it was Lady Gaga, a club remix at max volume.

Usually I would throw a pillow at Luke, miss him by six inches, roll over, and go back to sleep. Today as he lifted his t-shirt to wipe his face and then did a goofy dance to the song's refrain, I sat up and fixed my eyes on him.

"Turn it off," I called out, loud enough for Luke to hear me.

"Huh?" Luke lifted both hands to pop out his headphones, and when they dangled on his chest, they blared even louder.

"Turn the music off," I said.

Then Luke got the full brunt of the ferocious vampire

stare, which I'd been perfecting in my mom's makeup mirror for three days. It was designed to either (a) melt him into a puddle of his own sweat, or (b) make him totally obedient to me. Initially it worked in the second respect. Luke met my eyes and came over to my bed. It was working! My powerful gaze was pulling Luke over to me. My powerful gaze was powerful! Then Luke sat on my bed and told me:

"You have that crusty stuff in your eyes."

Luke reached toward my face. I lifted my arm to block him, but my vampire reflexes hadn't kicked in yet, and I was too slow. Luke poked me in the eye.

After Luke left for practice, my mother came in with the Dirt Devil, which I knew meant she wanted to have a heart-to-heart. She sat down on my bed and asked, "Is anything wrong, Finbar?"

I raised an eyebrow skeptically, but then I remembered I was practicing vampire habits. What would Chauncey Castle say?

"Is anything right?" I asked dramatically in return.

"Finbar." Now my mother's eyes narrowed and she gripped the cross at her neck like she was in distress. "Are you on drugs?"

"What does it matter what I am on?" I asked her. "All that matters is what I am...."

"FINBAR!" my mother shrieked, popping up off the bed. "YOU'RE ON DRUGS!"

This Chauncey Castle dialogue didn't work so well in real life. Maybe there's a reason *Publishers Weekly* called the book "skanky trash."

"I'm not on drugs, Mom," I said. "Where do you even come up with this stuff?"

"You're moody, you're not talking to any of us, and you're eating less," my mother said, then took a deep breath. "Are you doing pot?"

"Mom, if I were doing pot, I would be eating *more.*"

My mother aimed the Dirt Devil at my chest and switched it on, sucking on my black pajama shirt.

"Only someone doing pot would know that!" she yelled over the vacuum's roar.

After my mom left, I finally hopped out of bed. I took advantage of Luke's absence to perform an important pre–First Day of School task: decide what I was going to wear.

How was I going to dress like a vampire? I had a pretty lousy history of trying to convince people I was someone other than who I was. Look at my childhood Halloweens. Every year I'd start in August, brainstorming the scariest costume possible. A ghost, or a zombie, a mummy, or an ax murderer. When my neighbors opened the door, I'd growl, I'd wield a knife, I'd rage, I'd roar like the entire Broadway cast of *The Lion King.*

Still, when those Hoosier moms saw me, they'd always say, "Hi, Finbar. How are you?"

The best I ever got was a halfhearted "Aren't you scary?" But that was usually followed by the kind of *aww* sound you make when you find a puppy chewing your shoe. Other neighbors, knowing how to win my mother's heart, were too busy to be scared by me because they were taping a Bible passage to an Almond Joy. Almond Joys are already the world's suckiest candy without sores and plagues strapped to them. Pretty soon I'd be hauling half the New Testament door-to-door like a Jehovah's Witness.

So how would I ever pull off this vampire stuff?

I was lousy with violence. So I wouldn't be doing what made vampires vampires: I wouldn't be biting people. Luke had tried that back in the day, and it got him kicked out of Montessori school. My glamouring had no effect on my brother, so I wouldn't be hypnotizing people. I was certainly not Chauncey Castle when it came to seducing people. And I still didn't fully understand vampire attitude. So I had no choice but to work on my vampire look. In the hour left before Luke came back, I scrambled around the upstairs of our house, collecting all the sinister-looking clothes and accessories my family possessed. This included a black polo shirt Luke had since we were eight, a black button-up shirt that was too cool for my dad to wear, and a necklace of my mom's that I thought was a fang but turned out to be Luke's baby tooth on a string.

The necklace was ruled out first, obviously. Then I pulled the black polo shirt over my head. And believe me, that was not easy. That thing was *tight*. I looked like I should be raving at a club on the Jersey Shore. Except I couldn't raise my hand above my head to rave because when I did, the sleeve ripped.

The polo shirt was out.

Next I put on my dad's button-front shirt. It was kinda long on me (I'm pretty tall, but my dad, Tall Paul, is six-three). So when I tucked it in, the shirttail made a pretty nice bulge in the crotch of my jeans. That couldn't be bad. Plus, the shirt was black, mature, and pretty vampy-looking. In my mom's full-length mirror, I turned sideways and then turned the shirt collar up. Whoa. Too vampy. Like Count Whoever on Sesame Street. *ONE ass-kicking for Finn at his new school if he wears this shirt, TWO ass-kickings for Finn...mwah-ha-ha.*

Then, as I removed the bulge from my pants, I had an epiphany.

Vampires don't care about what shirt they wear. Vampires don't care about making impressions on the first day of school. Vampires don't care about all the stupid little stuff that the Finbar Frames of the world care about, like being the first one out in gym class dodgeball, facing rejection by girls, and being mocked for carrying SAT flash cards in their pockets. Vampires don't care that they can't flaunt their tans at the beach, that they get stared at, that they're different. Vampires don't care what other people think. And *that* is vampire attitude.

At St. Luke's, I always got to class before the second bell, which showed I cared about my grades. My name was always on the honor roll and the bylines of the school newspaper, which showed I cared about our school. I didn't go to keg parties, which might seem uncaring, but which actually meant that I cared so much what other people thought of my dancing and my lack of beer tolerance that I didn't dare show my face. I'd spent two years' allowance buying snails for Celine and then chased her down the street because I cared too much. That's why I'd ruined our date. And that's why I'd never dated, kissed, or even danced with a girl. I cared too much about what they thought of me.

Well, the caring stopped now.

I threw Luke's shirt and my dad's shirt in the hamper. I got rid of Luke's creepy tooth. I pulled my black pajama t-shirt back over my skinny white chest. For the rest of the day and that night, I wore that plain t-shirt. I wore it the next morning as I grabbed a piece of toast and ignored my mother's plea that I should drink green tea (she'd been watching Dr. Oz). As I climbed into my Volvo and headed for my new high school, that same black shirt I'd been wearing for three days conveyed it all—coolness, apathy, and a little bit of BO.

chapter

What had I been thinking? I was a complete idiot.

It was easy to brave at home. At home I was bolstered by my little bookshelves and my mother's blind love for her freakish offspring. It was easy to be brave and make plans when all I had to do was read a few books, survive an attack of solar urticaria, or absorb radiation from five hours of television. It was easy to make plans to seduce and impress everyone I knew when I knew no one in New York besides the three people obligated by law to love me: my mother, who gave birth to me; Luke, who shared my DNA; and my father, who didn't know any better.

Now, driving to Pelham Public High School in my Volvo, I felt completely intimidated. Even my little silver car was cowed by the other bigger, beefier cars—the SUVs and Jeeps with their iffy safety regulations and that one yellow Hummer that didn't give a shit about the environment. I tried to turn into the parking lot, but I got cut off by a red car whose driver was blasting gunshot sounds from a rap song. Ten minutes into public school and I'd already been in a drive-by!

Apparently I have an "I'm a pussy—cut me off" bumper sticker that I don't know about, because after that first car cut me off, all these kids on bikes crossed the street in front of my car without looking. As I let them pass, for so long that I shifted into park, I reflected that it might be the diversity that was making me nervous about this whole new-school thing. After all, I am from the Midwest. According to Wikipedia, my hometown of Alexandria, Indiana, has a population made up of "0.46% Black or African-American" people. Our neighbors were so excited when a black family moved in that they got them a welcome basket with the first three seasons of *The Cosby Show* on DVD. Back in Indiana, I went to school with a bunch of other white dudes in red vests and khakis. Most of them looked like me. And one of them was my twin brother.

But no one looked alike at Pelham Public High School. And you can bet your ass no one wore a tie. I parked my car in the farthest parking space from the school and got ready to hike the rest of the way. I didn't want to take a closer spot, in case it was reserved for seniors or other students or something. And looking around, there were a lot of other students I wouldn't want to mess with.

There were guys—guys with earrings, guys in tight jeans, guys with jeans around their thighs, guys who could fit my skull in their hands, guys who were bigger, tougher, tanner,

73

and cooler than me. And there were girls—girls in spaghetti straps, girls in tight jeans, girls making statements, girls clinging to groups, girls rummaging in enormous bags, girls whose ponytails moved independently of their bodies (they must be witches to make them do that!), girls with sunburns, girls smiling so brightly I couldn't look directly at them.

Trying to avoid eye contact with 150 kids at once, I slipped into the wave of movement toward the front door of the school.

"Hey!" a punk guy called from the hood of a rusted Chevy. One other guy was sitting there with him; another was sitting on the roof. They were sharing a cigarette, and all three were marking up their white sneakers with Sharpie pens.

I looked around me, then called back, "Hey."

"Nice choice of parking spot," the kid said.

All three laughed and looked down at my super-safe Volvo, which was chillin' with its airbags, with a space the size of an Olympic pool between it and the next car.

I shrugged.

"Fag," he called out to me.

As I cut from the student parking lot to the front of school, I saw my vampire plan through the eyes of all the different kids around me. And, through their eyes, my plan seemed really, really dumb. *This guy was going to pretend to be a vampire to be popular!* I imagined these kids whispering this to each other, posting it on Pelham Public's version of a Gossip Girl website. Despite their diversity, all of them would join together to laugh at me.

My head fell down to my chest, Eeyore-style. Same sad, slumping Finbar. And, apparently, same uncoordinated, doofus Finbar—because when I wasn't looking where I was going, I tripped over something. Actually, someone.

Perched like a gargoyle on the third-highest step, this girl pulled herself indignantly away from a large paperback book.

"You kicked me!" she squeaked, squinting up at me.

"Sorry," I said. "I'm so dumb. I'm sorry. It's my first day here, and I really have no idea where I'm going or what I'm doing, so…"

"Are you a freshman?" the girl asked. "I'm Jenny."

"No, I'm not a—"

"You're really tall for a freshman," Jenny said. "What are you, like six-two? You might be a whole foot taller than me. Let's do back-to-back."

When Jenny stood up to compare our heights, her book dropped to the steps. There were people rushing by us, so I stooped quickly to pick it up and prevent its being stepped on. The cover had a woman in a white dress that was somehow familiar—a white, lacy, cleavage-baring dress. And those large, drippy, overdramatic letters called to me. *Bloodthirsty*.

Jenny liked vampires! I straightened all the way up and handed her the book. Suddenly all these different people around me represented nothing more than different brands of inferiority. By God, I was the Chauncey Castle of Pelham Public High School! Guys wielding Sharpie markers from crappy cars and girls with scary-heeled shoes had nothing on me.

"I should get inside," I told Jenny, adding offhand but clearly, "I don't do well in the sun."

When I said that, Jenny looked super intrigued. Without even trying, I'd met the perfect target. Jenny followed me inside, almost tripping over herself to follow me. She followed me to the office, where I got my locker number, and to my locker, where I had to kick in the door to get it open. The whole time she followed me, Jenny asked me questions.

What grade was I? Junior. She was, too. Where had I moved from? Far away. But...where exactly?

"You know, the middle of the country," I said.

I wanted Vampire Finbar to emulate Chauncey Castle in his vague and philosophical answers to questions. Unfortunately, I ended up sounding like Justin Bobby from *The Hills.*

Jenny continued her interrogation: What classes was I taking? (I handed her my schedule. We compared classes.) Did I have a driver's license? Yes. Did I have a car? Yes. Did I like to read? Yes, very much. Did I ever read fantasy books? No. Why didn't I?

"I just don't think..." I snatched *Bloodthirsty* out of her hand. I glanced briefly at the lurker on the cover.

"I just don't think they're very realistic." I capped that off with a meaningful look.

I hoped Jenny would get the hint—that fantasy books weren't as real as my own life as a vampire. But she was too busy leading me to our first class in common, AP U.S. history. I was pumped to learn that, unlike St. Luke's, Pelham Public didn't give us assigned seats (no Johnny Frackas for me here!). Jenny chose a seat in the back and slid easily into it, and I squeezed myself into the seat next to hers. Since my summer growth spurt, I found my knees banging against tables and now my school desk. I was making legroom for myself when a kid sat down on the other side of Jenny. Apparently Pelham kids didn't care about who sat with whom, because he didn't even look before dropping his bag there.

"Hey, Jen," he said mildly. Promptly he went to sleep.

I slid forward to stare at this kid. I was fascinated. I'd never seen a real person fall asleep in class. I thought only seventies sitcom characters and John Hughes antiheroes did that. But there was an AP student, his curly Jewfro rising and falling in peaceful rhythm. He was, legitimately, asleep. I even saw a little bit of drool! As our teacher came into class, young and eager to fumble with the whiteboard and his laptop for twenty minutes to show us a two-minute Jon Stewart clip, I observed that guy's desktop nap and took it as an omen. A good sign that Pelham Public would be, at least compared with St. Luke's, a relaxed place.

Although Jenny was helpful, and I sat with her in my first two classes, I wasn't sure I wanted everyone to think we were best friends. She was a little strange, with her enormous collection of fantasy books stored in her L.L.Bean backpack and strapped to her back at all times. With orange hair and freckles, Jenny should have looked like a little kid in a graham cracker commercial. But she wore all black—black choker necklace and a black shirt with skulls and knives on it. And she had dyed her hair black too, although the orange hair had grown back in, so it was half-orange and half-black. As vampire companions go, she had the creepy goth look down but was kind of missing that sexy, cool edge I needed.

So in physics, our third class, I separated from Jenny to sit alone at a lab table and brood. Because the same group of kids had been in all three of my classes so far, and it was clear that all of us AP students would be spending a lot of time together, it was important to make a vampiric impression on them. So while our teacher built a model roller coaster out of Legos, I did my best Edward-Cullen-in-biology-class impression. When a pretty brunette girl sat down next to me, I only glanced at her briefly before looking away. I was sure this dark and sinister look would have the same effect on this girl as Edward's had on Bella in *Twilight*. My smoldering, angry eyes and bitter expression told her that I was an animal who could barely control my urge to lunge at her bare neck.

Obviously sucked in by my allure, the girl turned to me and spoke.

"Do you need some Pepto?" she asked me.

In my confusion, my mouth dropped open and I kinda lost my smoldering look.

"What?" I asked.

She pulled a bottle of Pepto-Bismol out of her bag, then told me, "You look like you're going to vom."

"What?" I asked.

"Vomit," she clarified.

After this incident, I decided not to venture out on my

own as much. I trusted Jenny to give me the necessary information about everyone.

The brunette? "That's Ashley Milano. She participates too much. And talks too much. And she abbrevs."

"She what?"

"She talks in abbreviations," Jenny told me. "Okay, next up, that's Jason Burke. He looks like a jock, but he's actually pretty smart.

"Matt Katz." Jenny pointed to the kid who'd fallen asleep in U.S. history. "Stoner kid. He's pretty cool. He knows more about the rap wars than Ms. Karl knows about centrifugal force."

Matt Katz didn't look like someone who would know about rap battles. He looked like someone who would camp out at a Dave Matthews concert and share a joint to "Satellite." Then again, I didn't look like a rap fan myself. Of course, I wasn't as intense as Matt, who apparently had a five-point thesis to prove that Tupac was still alive.

"Nate Kirkland," Jenny continued, pointing to a kid with surfer hair. Her description was brief: "Nosepicker."

"Really?" I asked. Picking your nose in class seemed a very bold move to me. Even bolder than sleeping in class.

"Well, he picked his nose once in third grade," Jenny said.

"How do you know that?" I asked.

"We've all gone to school together forever," she told me. "We haven't had a new kid in three years. We all find you... very *mysterious*."

Automatically, I smiled in delight. My plan was working! Then I remembered that mysterious guys—and vampires— didn't smile. So I generated a very manly frown.

"That's Kayla Bateman." Jenny continued her introductions, rolling her eyes at this one.

I looked over. Oh, I'd already noticed Kayla Bateman.

"She's always drawing attention to her boobs," Jenny said bitterly.

Now, Kayla was talking to some spellbound guys about the necklaces she was wearing. She fished one, then the other, out of her fathomless cleavage.

"My dad gave me the Star of David, and my mom gave me the cross," Kayla was saying. "But it's, like, why can't I have *both* of them on my chest?"

"Uh-huh." The two boys she was talking to nodded, mesmerized by her two…necklaces.

Gym was a pleasant surprise. And I've never said that in all my years of secondary education. When I arrived, there was a coach sitting at a table and about sixty-five kids lined up in front of him with their backpacks on. As each student came away from the table, they sat on the ground and filled out paperwork. This looked more like the DMV than physical fitness. And actually, I prefer the DMV to gym class.

I joined the long line and asked the girl in front of me, "Is everyone in sixth-period gym? There's, like, seventy of us in this line."

That would be a hell of a dodgeball game. I imagined sixty-nine people against me. I'd get creamed.

"There's only, like, twenty people in each rotation," the girl said. "Or maybe thirty in flag football. All those guys lined up early so they could get in the flag football rotation."

"Wait, so you're saying we can choose which activity we want to do?" I asked her.

When I got to the front of the line, the gym teacher barked at me: "Name?"

"Frame, sir."

For some reason, these guys always elicit a "sir" from me.

"Frame. Right, Frame." He handed me a lock closed around a hole-punched index card. "Locker number and combination."

Then he gave me a creased yellow sheet from a large stack.

"This is the list of rotations. Mark your first and second choice. And sorry to say..."

The coach slashed a big red X across the first choice on the sheet. Gym teachers got red pens, too?

"...flag football is all filled up."

"Gosh darn it," I said. That was my lame attempt to act upset. Really, I was pleased. Flag football always resulted in everyone grabbing at everyone else's crotch.

Yellow sheet in hand, I sought an open spot on the gym floor. There I sat, legs crossed, perusing my options. *Weight Training.* No way in hell. *Soccer.* Eh. *CardioPump, CardioFunk, CardioFlex...* embarrassing. *Nutritional Science?*

"Shit, man. All that's left is Nutritional Science," one guy leaving the line told another. Both guys sat down next to me.

"Hey, what is that?" I asked. "Nutritional Science?"

"You sit in a classroom and talk about vegetables," the guy told me. "You even have tests. It sucks."

"Yeah, sounds bad," I said.

Tests? I loved tests! I was great at tests! Folding my paper over so they couldn't see, I wrote a huge number 1 next to *Nutritional Science.* I creased the paper in half and slipped it into the pile on the coach's table.

The first day went so well that, by the time it was over, I had forgotten the one rough patch—homeroom. In fact, I didn't remember it until now, when I'm remembering everything.

Eff the *F* homeroom. It's always a terrible place. For fifteen minutes between first period (history) and second period (physics) I was plunged into a boiling pot of kids from all different cliques, with the only thing we had in common being *F* last names. Our homeroom teacher was Mr. Pitt.

"Frame?" Mr. Pitt, who was more pit stains than Brad Pitt, squinted at his attendance sheet.

"Is that Frame? Where's Frame?"

I tried to hide behind two kids playing hacky sack between the desks.

"Uh...uh," I stuttered. Then I remembered I was a vampire and stood up proudly.

"That's me," I declared.

"It's Frame? First name?" Mr. Pitt squinted at his sheet.

"Frame, last name," I said.

"So it's Finbar?"

"Right."

I sat at my desk.

"Jesus," said a lacrosse player next to me. "What kind of gay name is that?"

His friend, who was wearing one of those white baseball caps that's never seen a washing machine, gave a dumb laugh.

I waited with forced calm until Lacrosse turned around to check on my reaction.

The old Finbar would have turned red from embarrassment. Now, as Vampire Finbar, I retained my pasty serenity and focused by unwrapping a stick of Doublemint. Gum was also part of my plan. Somehow, gum chewing and coolness are associated in my mind.

When he turned toward me, I had a better view of the lacrosse player's rampant acne. Every lacrosse player I've met has been covered in zits. Neutrogena must be making a fortune off those cagey helmets.

"No answer, kid?" Lacrosse prodded. "What kind of gay name is that?"

I pointed toward a particularly ripe zit on his chin. It had two half-moon indents where he'd clearly tried to pop it with his nails but hadn't succeeded.

"You have something on your face...right there," I said.

God bless his friend's stupidity. He gave that same stuttering laugh to my comment as he had to Lacrosse's.

"Shut up, dude," Lacrosse muttered vaguely, to one or to both of us.

The bell rang. Homeroom torture was over and I felt different than I had before, when mocked. At St. Luke's, I'd always scrunched up in my seat, slumped over, or shrunk back. Today, I felt tall.

chapter

Upon first impression, Pelham Public looked just like I assumed it would be from Matt Katz's first-day-of-school nap: relaxed. But there was bullying going on—more than the snide remarks about my name.

During my second week at my new school, I left physics class early to get my lab notebook and saw this kid Chris Cho from my Nutritional Science class in the empty hallway. Cho is a freshman, but he's so skinny and small he looks like a lost middle schooler. He has one of those faces that always looks sad, but this period he looked even more bummed than usual. Then I saw that he wasn't alone in the hallway—he was with Chris Perez.

Chris Perez was a sophomore with a shaved head. Girls went crazy for him—partly because he was good-looking and partly because he was a badass. Everyone called him Perez. Everyone talked about him. I mean, I'd only been here a week and a half, and I'd heard several legends about him already. Perez had parked in the teachers' parking lot. Somehow he'd convinced the principal to let him keep the spot. Perez had climbed to the top of the rope in gym class. Perez had set off the fire alarm. Perez had bigger balls than anyone at Pelham Public. *He was notorious at Pelham because he got in trouble a lot.* Wait, correction—he *should* have gotten in trouble a lot. But when teachers caught him marking up the desks with ink pens or stealing from the school store, he'd play the sympathy card. He'd tell an elaborate story about his parents crossing the border and struggling to speak English, and he would get off scot-free.

But Perez didn't seem like a sympathetic character now. He swaggered up to Chris Cho and nudged him in the ribs with his fist.

"Hey, buddy!" Perez said in a loud, unpleasant voice that let me know he wasn't Cho's "buddy" at all.

Cho lowered his head and tried to walk past Perez down the hallway. But Perez sidestepped easily and blocked Cho's way.

"Nuh-uh-uh." Perez shook his head. "Gotta pay the toll."

Cho looked up with a blank face. I was watching from my locker down the hall, but Perez moved so quickly toward Chris Cho that I didn't know what had happened until I saw Perez hold Cho's wallet up above his head.

"Let's see what we have in here," Perez said. Lowering the leather wallet, he pulled it open with both hands. "Ten… eighteen bucks. Not bad today, Cho."

Perez removed five bills from Cho's wallet before letting

it drop to the floor. He folded the bills in half and put them in his pocket. Then he clapped Cho on the shoulder like a teammate and walked away.

As I walked past Cho, he was picking up his wallet from the hallway floor. I reminded myself that vampires didn't care about petty human interactions. I was a vampire, therefore I didn't care about what was happening to Chris Cho. I didn't feel bad for him—or feel empathy for him—at all.

In Jenny Beckman, I had my first female friend.

Being close to a girl—I mean, literally being within three feet of a girl—was new to me.

The motto at St. Luke's dances was "Leave room for the Holy Spirit." Our dean and chaperones would tell this to any guy who was dancing too close to a girl. I'm not sure anyone was concerned about the Holy Spirit being there as much as they were worried about St. Luke's guys rubbing their khaki boners all over those poor girls. As for the Holy Spirit, I'm pretty sure if He could be anywhere in Heaven or on Earth, He would not have chosen to sweat it out beneath that lame disco ball and spill Kool-Aid down his dress shirt like the rest of us.

I was never told to "Leave room for the Holy Spirit." Of course, I'd attended only two dances at St. Luke's—the first one freshman year, when I was hopeful about meeting girls, and the last one sophomore year, when I collected tickets. I didn't dance at either one, and I actually got closer to a girl when I was collecting tickets. I shared the ticket table with a suspicious student government leader from St. Mary's who accused me of stealing from the cash box. I recounted the crumpled five-dollar bills and cigarette butts in the cash box while, in the center of the dance floor, Luke yelled himself hoarse and pumped his fist in a circle of girls. Luke is unafraid to look like an idiot, so he's a great dancer. He's also unafraid to get physically close to girls, which is the main reason I've avoided dancing for sixteen years.

Now I had Jenny around, all the time, with no room for the Holy Spirit. I got to see all her quirks and emotions up close and personal. And Jesus, she had a lot of emotions.

"I can't believe Kayla Bateman got out of gym today," Jenny was saying. "It's, like, put on a *sports bra*. I'm pretty sure you can play dodgeball with big boobs. They're, like, extra protection."

Kayla Bateman apparently has some medical condition where her boobs won't stop growing. It's, like, a type of gigantism for boobs. She's the Andre the Giant of boobs. Although I'd seen Kayla talking to our male gym teacher, and I'm pretty sure it wasn't the doctor's note that got her out of class.

After three weeks of friendship, I had already decided that a lot of Jenny's frustrations in life derived from the fact that Kayla Bateman had enormous boobs and Jenny had no boobs. Well, not *no* boobs. I definitely still would have looked if she flashed me. Jenny had *small* boobs. Jenny would never admit that she was jealous of Kayla, but I picked up on it anyway. I have more sensitivity than the average male Clearasil user.

Personally, I thought a great solution would be to take

some of Kayla Bateman's boobs and give them to Jenny. Like, just lipo-suck Kayla's chest and inject it into Jenny's. It was the perfect solution. The girl who had too much would give to the girl who had too little. It was a redistribution of resources—a sort of Boob Communism. Boob-unism. Jenny would be happy with bigger boobs, and Kayla's chiropractor would probably be glad that she wasn't hauling those things around anymore.

Thinking about boobs in abstract economic terms was nothing new for me. I'd thought about boobs in more contexts than Karl Marx thought about poor people. But talking about boobs with someone who *had* boobs (even small ones like Jenny's)—I'd never done that at all. That was revolutionary!

But I had to remember there were both boys and girls at this school. We were swimming around in a pool of our own hormones and pheromones. There was sex everywhere. Even between the students and the teachers! This one teacher, Mrs. Anderson, had senior boys coming to her classroom every period to propose to her. It was all because she had these perfect, round breasts. Those breasts were the subject of much speculation in our school—namely, were they real or fake? Jason Burke was assumed definitive when he declared Mrs. Anderson's breasts "too good to be true."

Jenny wasn't my only friend at Pelham Public. It was hard not to get to know the other people she had introduced, considering I had seven classes a day with most of them. During our first physics lab period, Jason Burke asked me to be his partner.

"I didn't want Ashley Milano," Jason explained.

Not the most flattering motive for friendship. But good to know I ranked over Ashley Milano...and Nate the Nosepicker.

Ashley Milano, in turn, called out to me one day as I walked into AP literature.

"Finn, sit your ass down," she called to me. "You have to hear this story."

Someone has noticed me! I thought joyfully. Someone had noticed me...and my ass! Even with Jason, Kayla, Matt Katz, and Jenny there, Ashley's audience wasn't complete. She needed me, too.

As Ashley Milano's story—which, like most of her stories, involved a senior boy and speculations about rhinoplasty—dragged on, I realized I was so busy actually making friends that I kind of forgot to be distant and mysterious. I mean, I'd planned the whole vampire thing to give a reason why I didn't fit in with everyone else; why I wouldn't make friends; why I would be so different. But I wasn't that different, and I was starting to make friends. Dammit! My plan was foiled!

To keep myself on track, when Ashley Milano's story dragged on, I locked my creepy eyes on her face and tried to "glamour" her into shutting up. Concentrating intensely, I visualized her lips coming together, magically sealed by my will. If Vampire Finbar shut Ashley Milano up, Vampire Finbar would be hailed as a hero. Hell, even a superhero.

It worked for half a second. She stopped the story to say, "Ew, Finn, are you looking down my shirt?"

Yeah, right. With Kayla Bateman two feet away? No chance. But clearly I had to work on my glamouring. In fact, I had to work on my vampire plan as a whole. My planned tactic had been to convince Jenny that I was a vampire first, then have *her* tell everybody else. Jenny was perfect: she was a big fantasy fan, she was a little needy, and she had once conducted a séance and set her hair on fire, so she obviously believed in crazy stuff. But Jenny had foiled my plan by becoming my friend. She was around too much. Vampires didn't do these petty little human things like, say, eat or breathe. The eating I could handle—I didn't have the same lunch period as Jenny, and I wasn't very tempted by the frozen hamburgers in the unrefrigerated vending machines near the student lounge. The breathing, though? I couldn't really kick that habit. And I actually tried, too.

But Jenny wasn't getting the hint. And I certainly wasn't going to tell her outright, "I'm a vampire." Due to her fantasy obsession, I had been waiting for her to confront me with, "You're a vampire, aren't you? I know you are!" and let me give my mysterious Chauncey Castle shrug. But she wasn't confronting me.

Another reason I stalled in my vampire quest was this: I met a girl.

For my first week and a half at Pelham Public, I didn't brave the cafeteria at lunch, retreating to my favorite place, the library, instead. Because I was the only junior taking AP

Latin with the Pelham Public seniors (which was due to my sadistic Catholic teachers and their love of Latin declensions), I didn't have lunch with any other juniors. I had lunch fourth period, when most of the sophomores and some freshmen ate.

My first day in the cafeteria, I saw a girl sitting by herself at a table, reading a book. This made me incredibly suspicious. Why? Because I thought it was a Finbar-trap. Mousetraps have cheese in them, and Finbar-traps would have shiny-haired high school brunettes in them, reading *New York Times* Notable Books.

Despite my suspicious instincts, I drew closer to this girl. And I felt the way my mother must have felt when she fell in love with my father through all those hockey pads and that face mask. I loved this girl even from the back, when all I could tell about her was that she had a hell of a great shampoo and had passed every scoliosis test she'd ever taken. I had to go up to her. I *had* to approach her. This need was bigger than my self-consciousness and my lack of experience with girls and my fear that I would spill my cafeteria spaghetti on her, which was basically the worst thing you could spill on someone.

When the girl turned, she was beautiful. She had glasses on, and behind them she had eyelashes you could count one by one like spider's legs, and brown eyes taking in great big gulps of everything around her. Then she turned back to her book, which, as I walked up to her, I could see was *Life of Pi*, by Yann Martel.

"The guy lives," I told her. "But Richard Parker dies."

Life of Pi is about a shipwreck survivor who ends up floating on a lifeboat in the middle of the ocean. He's stuck there with a giant tiger from the zoo, the tiger being named Richard Parker. The big suspenseful hook of the story is if the guy will survive in the boat, be saved, or be eaten by the tiger. Then he gets to be friends with the tiger, so you wonder if the tiger's gonna survive. I'd just spoiled the story for this girl.

One side of her mouth curled up. I'm impressed by people who can do one-sided things, like raise one eyebrow. This, on this girl, was even better. She had great lips.

"I know," she said.

"Oh... I'm, uh, sorry."

I fumbled for an apology, ironic because she'd just told me I *hadn't* ruined her ending. But I'd anticipated that she would be surprised by my comment, not me by hers.

The girl smiled, but turned back to *Life of Pi*. I felt the full awkward weight of my own body hovering over her. Say something or leave, Finbar. Fight or flight.

"Read it before?" I asked. I was suddenly obnoxiously loud because I was excited by the possibility that she *could* have read it before. The only thing better than a girl who read books was a girl who read the same book twice. A rereader. This girl could be a rereader!

"What?" When the girl looked up, her short dark hair fell into her eyes.

"Is that why you knew? The end?" I explained.

"I read the last page first," she whispered, leaning a little toward me. Then she ducked behind her own falling bangs, like she was ashamed of having ruined the ending for herself.

"Unacceptable." I shook my head. "I'm ashamed of you, Miss..."

Turning her head to get her bangs out of her eyes, the girl flipped the book so it was facedown next to her lunch tray. That was a big move. I'd officially captured her attention more than a shipwreck and a tiger.

"Gallatin," she said. "Kate Gallatin."

Then she placed her hand on the place beside her at the table. And I sat down, as simple as that. Well, first I put my backpack down in an awkward place on the ground, and it blocked the back legs of the chair, so I tried to pull the chair out but failed, so then I moved my backpack, but my legs were in the way of the chair, so I stepped to the side, pulled out the chair, and *then* sat down. But basically, I sat down.

"I'm Finbar," I said. "I'm, uh, new."

Glamouring is very difficult with a gorgeous girl. I narrowed my eyebrows as I locked eyes with Kate for the first time, but then Ashley Milano's comment about me looking down her shirt popped into my head. I didn't want Kate to think that!

Luckily, Kate, like everyone else, ignored the intense, hypnotic stare I fixed upon her.

"I'm new, too!" she said. "I haven't seen you in my classes. Are you a sophomore?"

"No, uh, a junior," I told her.

"Oh," Kate said, grinning. "So you were held back in lunch?"

I laughed out loud. She was so quick. I would have to step up my game from "Uh," "Oh," and my own name.

"I just couldn't graduate to using forks," I said.

"Some guys can't handle their opposable thumbs." Kate shook her head.

Again I laughed, breaking that back-and-forth rhythm of our teasing each other. She picked up the slack, saying, "You're probably only allowed to eat finger foods. Too bad it's pasta day."

"Don't tell anyone I'm here," I joked. "Do you mind smuggling a fugitive?"

Kate smiled. Except for the way my ribs were closing in — like they were cave walls and my heart was Indiana Jones — this whole conversation made me feel like I'd known this girl forever.

Except, of course, if I'd known this girl forever, I wouldn't be a dour and cynical sixteen-year-old virgin who was pretending to be a vampire. But anyway…

"Actually," I said, "I have lunch this period because I'm taking a weird Latin class. I mean, uh…an advanced Latin class."

Maybe my knowledge of Latin was a really sexy quality.

"You would have been cooler if you stuck with the 'failing lunch' story," Kate told me.

Maybe not.

95

"Yeah, yeah," I said. "But am I cool enough to eat lunch with you?"

"You should," Kate said. "I'm great with this." She flourished her fork. "I could teach you a thing or two."

"We'll see, sophomore," I threatened, narrowing my eyes. Then I sat the whole lunch period with Kate, a smart, funny, literate, and incredibly sexy girl. I was so excited, I actually *did* forget how to use my fork.

For the rest of the afternoon, I was completely distracted. I was thinking about Kate. When Jenny came up to me at my locker, I barely registered that she was inviting me to go somewhere with her on Saturday afternoon. Still dreaming of Kate, fantasizing about doing a *New York Times* crossword puzzle together after blasphemous Sunday-morning sex, I agreed to whatever Jenny had asked me.

"Great!" Jenny said. "Don't worry, we don't have to wear costumes. And none of the weapons are real."

"Huh?"

I froze by my locker as Jenny trotted happily away. Either Jenny and I had been hired as entertainers for a *Lord of the Flies*–themed birthday party, or I'd just accepted an invite to an S&M orgy.

chapter

Late Saturday afternoon, I picked up Jenny in my Volvo, and we drove to the Seventeenth Biannual East Coast Fantasy Fest. To me, the convention center was like a zoo where the animals walked around free, shaking one another's hands and taking photographs together and drinking coffee. As I did when I was at the zoo, I wanted to look in too many different directions at once. Just when I'd focus on something new and strange, trying to understand it, some other thing would shimmer or flutter or screech by, and I'd turn my head. As a result, I bumped into about four different people—or creatures—within my first five minutes in the convention center.

There was a guy with horns the color of foreskin curled around his head who jumped out at me first. From a distance, the mask that covered his entire head was so similar to the color of his actual skin that it seemed an outgrowth of him.

Two men with beards down to their knees made peace signs at everyone who passed. A Round Table's worth of knights in full armor lifted their face guards to sip from cans of Diet Pepsi. An angry little gargoyle with cracking blue-gray body paint was crouching around the ground and I accidentally tripped over him.

"Watch it, bitch," he snapped.

"Jesus," I said to Jenny, pulling myself back on my feet.

"C'mon, not everyone's that mean," Jenny said.

She was right. A group of girls in cottonball blond wigs and flesh-colored bodysuits blew me kisses.

Awkwardly, I waved back at them.

"It's not as bad as you thought, is it?" Jenny asked eagerly.

A sweaty mustachioed man in slippers and a green Robin Hood hat lunged in front of us, brandishing a real and rusted sword. His foe was a six-foot-five man in a full-bodied felt dragon costume. The blade missed my aorta by about six inches.

"Whoa!"

I made a face at Jenny, like I was thinking, *It's worse than I thought*. But in reality, these crazy people around us both embarrassed and kind of impressed me. They embarrassed me because I couldn't imagine walking into a public place with some horned mask or body paint. I would never even tell two hundred strangers that I liked to read, much less that I liked to read books about witches and dwarves. I thought about how the standard high school boy writes "I don't read" under *Favorite Books* on his Facebook profile. Why? Because, whether it's true or not, that's the safe, conformist response. But not one of these Fantasy Fest-ers was a conformist, and they impressed me because of that. I was fascinated with the thought and time they'd put into their costumes, with the enthusiasm of Lord of the Rings fans debating metaphorical issues in Elvish, with the warmth of *Buffy the Vampire Slayer* Buffys embracing each other after months apart. One dedicated *Harry Potter* Dumbledore had grown a beard down to his knees. It must have taken him two years to grow that beard. Of course, he was, like, seventy years old. I guess by the time you're that old, you don't really care what people think of you. Or maybe none of these fantasy fans cared what people thought of them. Maybe that was what impressed me—their ability to put the weird things about themselves out in the open.

Speaking of people who put weird things about themselves out in the open, Jenny was tugging me across the convention center. She'd come to the Fantasy Fest mostly to get her book signed by Carmella Lovelace, the author of *Bloodthirsty*. Unfortunately, she wasn't the only *Bloodthirsty* fan in attendance. When we turned the corner, we saw a hundred-person line. About fifteen percent of those people were girls dressed in slutty white dresses to look like Virginia White.

When one Virginia with lame cleavage saw the book in Jenny's hand, she said, "Better get in line, girl."

"We've been here since noon," added another, who had ketchup down her dress as fake blood.

Jenny smacked me on the elbow as we headed for the back of the line.

"Ow! What?"

"We should have come earlier," she admonished me.

"I told you that I have a sun sensitivity," I told Jenny. "We couldn't come at noon."

"It's not even sunny today!" Jenny told me. "It's about to rain! And why are you so sensitive to the sun, anyway? What's up with that?"

A blond girl with hair like feathers jumped out of the line toward me. Because of my recent experience with the sword guy and the felt dragon, it was understandable that I jumped back and kind of shrieked like a girl.

"Hi!" she squealed. "How are you?"

The blond girl pulled me in for a hug, pinning my arms at my sides. Jesus, girls were really friendly at these things. Either that or my mom's notes were right and I was a stud.

When she pulled away, though, I saw it was the blonde from the train. The girl who had started all of this by mistaking me for a vampire. Apparently she had branched out beyond her own creepy vampire book, *Nocturnal Terror*, to the more sexy *Bloodthirsty*.

"How are you feeling?" Blondie asked in a low voice, leaning toward me.

Jenny listened intently.

"Oh, fine," I said politely. "How are you?"

"I'm sorry I called you out that day on the train," Blondie said in the same low voice. "I shouldn't have revealed what you were in a public place. I understand why you got so pissed. I'll be more subtle from now on."

"Oh, okay, well, thanks," I said, hoping Jenny was picking up possible hints from this, but more strongly hoping to escape this psycho.

"Are there any others here?" the blond girl hissed.

"What?" I asked.

"Other vamp—"

"No," I said quickly. "I mean..."

A boy, probably twelve years old, walked by sulkily with his hands in his pockets. He was dressed like Edward Cullen from *Twilight*—reddish streaks in his hair, all this powder on his face to make him pale.

"No *real* ones," Blondie finished for me, her voice low and intense.

"How do you guys know each other?" Jenny asked, looking up from me to Blondie like a child trying to decode a grown-up conversation.

"Does she know?" Blondie asked me.

Jenny looked up expectantly. I felt intensely awkward. I felt even less comfortable with the idea of telling Jenny my fake vamp status than I had in school. And explaining Blondie would force me to say it.

"We have to go to the back of the line," I commanded Jenny.

"Finbar!" Jenny wailed. "Carmella Lovelace just got here! I can see her beehive hair!"

"We should really..."

But it was too late. A jumpy brunette had joined my one-girl bleach-blond fan club.

"Is this him?" the brunette asked conspiratorially. She pointed to me, and I was startled to see that a rubber glove had transformed her hand into a large green claw.

"Shhh!" The blonde's hiss dissolved into giggles.

"This is him!" the clawed brunette called to another girl.

The third girl came towering over with frightening force. She was clearly the only Amazon woman in suburban New York. The girl had me by about five inches. Hell, she had Yao Ming by five inches.

"The vampire!" she hissed excitedly.

It was only when the Amazon bent at the waist to hug me, and I ducked, that I could see Jenny's reaction. Beneath her carrot-red roots and goth-black streaks, Jenny's mouth had dropped open. She held the cover of *Bloodthirsty* and looked from it to me. Her mouth didn't shut. Seriously, she could have swallowed a fly.

Meanwhile, I was in a frightening high school girl huddle, my eardrums flooded by high-frequency screams, dispossessed from my own body as it was examined like I was a Jonas Brothers impersonator at a suburban mall.

"Look at his skin!" one marveled, stroking my forearm.

Another grabbed the same arm from the first girl and flipped it over.

"You can see all of his veins," she said. Her manicured finger traced a blue line down into my palm.

A sense of déjà vu flooded me. When had this happened to me before? A crowd of girls pressing upon me, desperate to touch me? Oh, wait. That had never happened to me before. But it had happened to Luke. Maybe we had the twin ESP thing going. And clearly, both of us were very desirable.

But my smugness was fleeting. After six or seven girls lined up near me, feeding my ego, I saw the first guy.

My first thought was that he was joining the girls in admiring my body. Which I guess would be fine, as long as he looked and didn't touch. Then Jenny called out desperately:

"Finbar! Watch out!"

Oh, shit. Now I knew why there were guys coming after me. I had forgotten how close we were to the vampire slayers table. Apparently in this alternate universe, Buffy was not the only vampire slayer. There were also adolescent boys, and even full-grown men, who hated vampires. I knew this, because the vampire slayers table had a huge vampire doll hanging from a noose above the table. When last I passed, the guys at this table had been eagerly debating the merits of silver chains and wooden stakes as vampire-killing weapons. Now they had stopped talking theoretically. There was someone in their midst for whom they'd waited their whole fantasy lives: a real, live (well, dead, but you know) vampire.

And oh, shit—it was me!

I grabbed on to the biggest thing in sight to protect me— the Amazon girl. I actually felt pretty safe inside all those girls. Safe enough to peek around Blondie and see that the vampire slayers' wooden stakes were made out of cardboard. One of them even had "Best Buy" visible through a wash of brown paint. So these guys weren't going to *actually* kill me. I could calm down. The vampire slayers weren't that tough.

But there were more joining the ranks. All the Jacobs had come over from the Twilight table. In Stephenie Meyer's books, Jacob is a jocky high school dude. Now, that alone would have me waving a white flag. But Jacob happens to be a jocky high school dude...who turns into a WEREWOLF. And guess who happens to be the mortal enemy of the were-wolf? Who does Jacob want to hunt down in the woods and tear apart limb by pale puny limb?

The vampire.

Of course, these Jacobs couldn't really turn into werewolves. But they were charging at me like they thought they *could* turn into werewolves. And besides that, Jacobs were way cooler than vampire slayers. They were the kind of guys who came to a fantasy convention to collect weapons and hit on girls. And, you know, join a furious mob about to beat down a pale kid.

I turned and took off, frenzied, seeking the nearest exit sign. With the Jacobs involved, the mob was really gaining on me.

I slammed the door open, took a brief breath while surveying the parking lot, and then sprinted around the back of the building, panting like I'd just climbed Mount Gundabad.

"I have a compass!" I heard a vampire slayer say from around the front of the convention center.

Uh-oh. It was only a matter of time before they multiplied two pi by the radius of this building, which was a geodesic dome, and found me 180 degrees around the back. Wait, hold up. That's it! This building was a geodesic dome! (Okay, you're right, a guy who knows what a geodesic dome is shouldn't mock anyone for using the number pi. FYI—a geodesic dome is a building that looks like a golf ball.)

But I felt suddenly light and free. Because I had remembered this time the whole Alexandria fire squad had been called to our middle school because Luke had scaled a building and was camped out on top. The building he scaled was our indoor track, which was a geodesic dome. The fantastic thing about geodesic domes was that you could climb them.

Okay, not *anyone* could climb them. Luke could climb them, being the 80 percent ape that he is. It was a little more difficult for me considering I had zero climbing abilities and wasn't wearing a belt.

But I reached up the base of the dome and found a handhold, and then found a ledge for my foot. I began to climb, fueled by the need to escape the Jacobs and the vampire slayers and those *Bloodthirsty* fiends. For one thing, I'd never been in a fight in my life. For another, if I were in a fight, it would become clear I wasn't a vampire. I didn't have super speed, super strength, or any kind of physical coordination.

Plus, one extra nasty little detail: I'm scared of blood. I *hate* blood. That's one reason I try to avoid fights, violent team sports, and, come to think of it, *CSI* in any of its many incarnations. And, if I passed out at the sight of blood, everyone would know I was not a vampire. Being scared of blood wasn't exactly good for my street cred. Or whatever the vampire version of street cred was. Coffin cred?

Oh, why had I given in to fantasy violence? Why hadn't I brokered peace? Why hadn't I suggested, "Let's all join hands and sing the Ewok song from *Return of the Jedi*! All species are welcome here!" Why had I even come to this Fantasy Fest? Why had I decided that becoming a vampire would result in *less* people wanting to beat me up?

Too scared to climb down, I crouched on top of the geodesic dome for an hour and a half. Twenty minutes into that time, it began to rain. The whole time I was anxiously anticipating my reunion with Jenny, during which, I was 99 percent sure, she would ask me, "Are you a vampire?" Had I been better with vampire attitude, she would have gotten the message that I *was* a vampire but didn't want to talk about it. But I was never good at sending out cool and subtle signals — see my date with Celine for another example. Instead, all of my vampire behaviors and encounters so far, from my glamouring Ashley Milano's boobs to my mom's drug talk, had elicited the question, "What the hell is wrong with you, Finbar?"

I had set out to give an impression, to intrigue, to fascinate, to attract, even to seduce. I hadn't set out to lie. I would have to tell Jenny the truth. And then this whole thing would be over. This snobby poet T. S. Eliot once said, "This is the way the world ends — not with a bang but a whimper." This was how my vampire world ended — not with me getting banged, but with me on a weird roof, soaking wet, and with my pants sliding down my ass. Definitely reason to whimper.

When people started to leave the convention, I moved across the roof toward a position above the exit doors and watched people leave. Whoa. More than a few fantasy characters who had arrived separately were now going home together, looking pretty cozy. I didn't even want to think about what a guy in a fur coat and a girl with a goat's head would do on a first date. Oh, wait! There was Jenny!

"Jenny!" I hissed from my dome.

She looked up, puzzled.

"Jenny!" I hissed louder.

Then a group of vampire slayers headed to their car (wow, a new Land Rover. One of them must have a killer day job) and I ducked down again.

"We really scared the shit out of him!" one of the slayers said, highly satisfied. "Hell, yeah!" another agreed. They high-fived like jocks.

When the slayers had passed, I called, "Jenny! Help me down!"

"Finbar?" Jenny called. She stomped off the parking lot pavement and into the mud. She looked down miserably at her muddy shoes, and then furiously up at me.

"What the hell are you doing on the roof?" she yelled. "And why didn't you answer your cell phone?"

I pointed down to the ground by a skinny tree.

"My phone fell down," I told her.

Jenny looked up at me and raised an eyebrow.

"My pants fell down, too," I said uncomfortably, trying to hike my jeans up in a subtle way.

"Would you come down?" she asked me.

"I'm waiting for the Jacobs to leave!" I told her.

"They left," Jenny said. "They went off to eat some red meat or something. Come *down!*"

Jenny helped me down from the dome, and she dug my cell phone out of the mud. She even looked away when my damp jeans got caught on a rain gutter. As we dashed to my car in the rain and I unlocked the passenger door for her, I was thinking what a good pal Jenny was. That is, until I turned the key in the ignition and she wouldn't let me leave the parking spot. She locked her hand over mine around the gearshift.

"Tell me the truth," Jenny demanded dramatically, her voice even louder than the pounding rain on my Volvo.

"What?" I shoved my wet hair out of my face, avoiding her eyes.

"I mean, you're skinny," Jenny began. "You're pale. You can't go in the sun."

"Well, that stuff is all true," I told her. "But look, Jenny, I can't tell you..."

The words "I am a vampire" just couldn't form on my lips. My mother had drilled too many commandments and vivid images of the flames of hell into my head. Then, while I was reflecting on my Catholic inability to lie, divine inspiration struck.

"I can't tell you," I said with passion. "Because it would just be too dangerous."

If I told Jenny I was a vampire, I would burn in hell. Dangerous. If I told Jenny that I wasn't really a vampire, then word could get out that I was *pretending* to be a vampire, and surely someone would kick my ass for that. Dangerous.

Jenny's eyes were huge, her face serious. She nodded, heavy with the weight of my secret. Obviously, she believed it would be dangerous because I was, in fact, a vampire. She looked down in awe at my skin touching her skin.

"Your hand is freezing." She spoke slowly, as if under a spell. "Wow."

I nodded sadly, as if cold hands were a necessary part of my life...or my lack of life. I wondered, though, why my hands were actually so cold all the time. Maybe I should get that checked out.

Because I was covered in mud and had a tear in my pants, I came into my house through the back door. When I did, I found Luke with a nonstick spatula poised menacingly in his hand and half a cheeseburger hanging from his mouth.

"What the hell?" I asked. "Were you gonna hit me with that?"

"Sorry," Luke said. "I thought you were breaking into the house. Mom's paranoia is really contagious."

"Yeah, whatever, Hamburglar," I told him. "Where is Mom?"

"Seven thirty mass," Luke said. "Where were you? And... what *happened* to you?"

Because climbing a geodesic dome was Luke's idea, telling him about my dumb climb and my pants falling down and my phone getting all muddy might make me irrationally mad at him. So instead I decided it was time to tell him my secret. After all, my brother loved me. He would accept my new lifestyle choice. Sure, some people believed what I was doing was morally wrong. Some more conservative media portrayed us as evil menaces, preying on children, wooing others to our nasty way of life. But I was sure my brother would accept me as a vampire.

"What?" Luke asked when I told him. "How did this happen?" Then he narrowed his eyes like he did before mowing a rival down on the football field and asked, "Did someone bite you, bro?"

"I mean, I'm not *actually* a vampire," I told him. "This girl Jenny who I was with today, she thinks I'm one. So I just kind of ... went along with it."

"So supposedly," Luke said, "you're just walking around with the rest of us, but you're a vampire?"

"Yeah. That's the idea. I mean, that's her idea."

"What do you do about the fangs?"

"What?"

"Did she ever ask to see the fangs?"

"No!" I protested. "I'm a nice vampire!"

"Things like that pop out involuntarily," Luke said. "Like when Ms. Alexander tutored Sean O'Connor, and he got a huge—"

"All right," I interrupted. "But your fangs don't pop out involuntarily when you don't have them."

Luke stood there and thought for sixty seconds, which was a long time for him.

"You need to be faster," Luke decided.

"What?"

"Faster. Stronger." Luke began to sing Daft Punk by way of Kanye West. *"Harder, better, faster, stronger..."*

I gave Luke a disparaging look, one to prevent him from dancing.

"Look." Luke flung a quarter of his cheeseburger across the room for emphasis. "Vampires are fast. And strong. Like, abnormally fast and strong. Like, Usain-Bolt-meets-Incredible-Hulk. Get it?"

"Whatever, Luke, I'm fast."

"You need to be..." Luke clapped his hands and made a *whoosh* sound.

"No one's testing me on being a vampire," I said.

"I bet you a thousand dollars." Luke hopped up onto a kitchen chair. "You'll come to a vampire situation where you have to be fast."

How I wished I could raise one eyebrow at a time.

"And that's when you'll thank me," Luke said, grinning.

"Thank you for what?"

"Finbar Frame," Luke announced, "I am going to be your personal trainer."

"Jesus," I groaned. "You are not."

"I am," Luke said. "I'm going to be your personal trainer.

111

And you're going to be a *brick wall*. You're going to drive that vampire girl crazy...what's her name again? The vampire chick? Sookie?"

"Jenny," I said. "But she's not, like, *my* vampire girl...."

"A girl." Luke sighed nostalgically. "Jesus, Finn, you're spoiled. Fuck Fordham Prep. I haven't seen a girl in a year and a half!"

I decided that if Luke really made me work out with him, I would punish him by telling him all about Kayla Bateman and her unusual boobs. Then he'd really be jealous of me.

chapter

A combination of factors led me to use the word *cock* in my seventh-period AP literature class.

I'd been at Pelham Public for a month and a half now. And, for all that time, in the back of my mind I'd been ruminating about how sexual vampires were. I mean, isn't sex the reason the vampire trend has lasted so long? Back in the day, Dracula seduced all these pale, ruffly virgins. Now, Chauncey Castle's pale face glowers from *Bloodthirsty* posters on walls all over the country, fixed on teenage girls in their beds. And the girls love it.

Beyond the attraction factor, vampires are supposed to be really good at sex. Hence all of the talk about "the only thing harder and more powerful than Chauncey Castle's fangs." And hence all the action that made Virginia White's breasts "shiver," "quiver," and "tremble" in every damn chapter of that book.

Frankly, I didn't know what it *meant* to be good at sex. I'd always assumed my first sexual experience would be kinda like my trip to the Touch Tunnel in the Museum of Science and Industry. I'd plunge in blindly. I'd feel my way around while more experienced personnel watched and laughed from an infrared camera. And I'd hope to emerge before I ran out of oxygen.

In fact, I felt really uncomfortable with the idea of sex. It didn't help that, at St. Luke's, guys had this game where they would concoct ridiculous and fictional sexual terms, claim they were real but obscure, and taunt each other with them. Actually, usually they would taunt *me* with them, as I was a target who didn't have the balls to admit I didn't know what something meant. For example, Johnny Frackas would call across study hall:

"Hey, Fagbar, I bet you don't know what a pickle flip is."

A pickle flip? No, I didn't know. In my head I'd file furiously through every *Maxim* magazine I'd ever stolen, or try to picture pages of my anatomical encyclopedia. I'd rack my head generating possible moves and positions and perverse acts that could constitute a pickle flip.

Well, the verb *to flip* generally means to rearrange from facedown to faceup. Or vice versa. Or, used in a more gymnastic sense, *flip* could mean a full three hundred and sixty degree turn of the body. Like a somersault. *Pickle* was pretty obvious. Pretty alliterative. *Pickle* equaled, well, you know. But I couldn't do a somersault with my...

"Hey, guys!" Johnny Frackas would call out, interrupting

114

my lengthy pause. "Fagbar doesn't know what a pickle flip is!"

My face would turn red, and I wouldn't have anything to say in return. And why not? Because I assumed that every guy in the room knew something I didn't.

That was how a bunch of Catholic schoolboys taught me an important lesson about sex. All you have to do to make people think you know about sex is talk about it a lot.

Although I planned to put this theory into action and bring sex into a conversation—the more people in the conversation the better—I hadn't found the right opportunity yet. Whenever I was with a group of guys and girls from class and we broached that subject area, either some other guy made a dumb dirty joke and swiped my chance or I didn't notice the opening to bring up sex until it was too late. To be fair, I had been busy lately, and distracted, mainly by physical exhaustion.

Luke's training regimen was killing me. He woke me up every morning at 5:45 AM. Luke begins his own strength training by lifting 130 pounds—that is, by lifting 130 pounds of reluctant Finbar out of his warm bed. Then we both do cardio—running three friggin' miles around our neighborhood when only people dumb enough to own dogs are awake. Then it's back upstairs (and every step fucking *burns*. Why do our stairs have so many damn steps?). Then it's so much weight lifting you would think the two of us were filming a Total Gym infomercial in our bedroom. I'm not sure that my body is made for exercise. Since starting this whole thing with Luke, I'd suffered sunburn (yes, sometimes even before the sun rose. Life—and UV rays—are cruel), shin splints, a strained bicep, a twisted ankle, a sweat rash, and a groin pull. With that last injury, Luke tried to administer some first aid, and I think we accidentally violated some New York State incest laws.

I had also been getting busy because of Kate. No, not getting busy *with* Kate. Wrong preposition. But I had been getting a lot closer to her. We ate lunch together almost every day. She told me she wanted to start an investment club at our school.

"You can make money off these online stock market games!" Kate told me. "Well, if you beat those douche bags from the high school of economics."

Well, I definitely wanted to beat those douche bags from the high school of economics. Mostly so I could impress Kate. So I wasn't going to admit how bad I was at math. Math is supposed to be one of those things guys are good at. So I checked out *A Kid's Guide to Stock Market Investing* from the library. I also asked Matt Katz for advice, because apparently his dad was a successful investor.

"Sure, I'll ask Dad for some stock names," Matt Katz told me. "He's good. He earned so much last year he bought my stepmom a whole new face."

While Kate got me interested in the investment club and even made math a little bit sexy, I recommended books for her to read and admitted to her that I like poetry.

"Really?" She smiled. "I never knew a guy who liked poems."

Except for those homos from the Dead Faggots Society, I finished in my mind. That's what Johnny Frackas had called me after my poem was published in the *St. Luke's Lit*: "One of those homos from the Dead Faggots Society."

"Which poets are good?" Kate asked. "You should tell me which ones to read. Remember I'm a beginner."

"Yeats and Frank O'Hara are awesome," I began. "And H.D., and Jeffrey McDaniel is really funny and stuff. But if you like more traditional kinda rhymey stuff, definitely do Shakespeare's sonnets."

"Shakespeare?" Kate tilted her head with mock thoughtfulness. "Never heard of him."

"He's a pretty good writer." I grinned. "Doesn't get the respect he deserves."

And, actually, it was poetry that provided me with my sexual opening (haha). Mrs. Rove's introduction to our poetry unit gave me the opportunity to dirty-talk the pants off my seventh-period literature class.

On a dull rainy Tuesday in mid-October, our AP literature teacher announced, "This is Andrew Marvell's 'To His Coy Mistress.'" Mrs. Rove kind of looked like Hillary Clinton, but she had this huge Escalade in the teachers' parking lot, so she must have had a secret gangsta side. Or a stockbroker husband.

My classmates turned their heads from the drug deal going down in the parking lot and groaned in remarkable unison. Even AP students hated the poetry unit. But me, I stopped doodling fangs in the margins of my looseleaf and looked up expectantly. This was my chance to dominate English class and flaunt my vampire intelligence and confidence. "To His Coy Mistress" was one of my favorite poems! Actually, it was part of my favorite genre of poems, which could be called Poems Guys Write to Get Girls to Sleep with Them. Maybe I like poetry for the same reason I like really clever rappers, like Nas and Talib Kweli and A Tribe Called Quest: because I secretly hope I can develop the verbal skills to seduce a woman. Sure, right now I can barely remember my name around hot girls like Kate, but I'm more likely to develop verbal skills than biceps.

"Mr. Kirkland, please pass on those poems," she called out. "Mr. Kirkland!"

Mr. Kirkland, aka Nate the Nosepicker, woke up and then passed the pile. He forgot to give himself a copy.

"Now that you've had a few minutes to read this over for a first impression," Mrs. Rove said, "can anyone tell me what this poem is about?"

Ashley Milano thrust her hand upward.

"Time's wing-udd chariot," Ashley Milano pronounced carefully. "That's a symbol! It stands for…like, how everyone's getting old really fast."

Ashley Milano knew symbols. Her intelligence stopped there, but she knew symbols.

"Great, Ashley. We'll definitely be discussing symbols later on," Mrs. Rove said. "But can anyone give me the general synopsis of the poem? What is the narrator saying? Why did he write this?"

Matt Katz gave a huge snore that pulled his head off his chest. It was so loud he woke himself up. Kayla Bateman was sighing loudly to advertise her frustration at not being able to button her cardigan over her chest. Jason Burke scratched a tic-tac-toe board onto the corner of his poem. Only Ashley displayed any interest—she was hunting down and viciously stabbing at symbols and metaphors with a red pen.

"What is the goal of this poem?" Mrs. Rove asked again.

Silence. I took a final survey of the room. No one was going to speak up.

So I spoke up, without even raising my hand.

"Sex," I said clearly.

Matt Katz's snore turned into a choking cough. Jason Burke reached over to clap him on the back. Two girls in the corner painting their nails with Wite-Out widened their eyes at each other and giggled. Ashley Milano's mouth dropped open. I'd never heard her be quiet for so long.

"Mr. Frame?" Mrs. Rove said.

She sounded stern, but I heard interest in her voice, too. She gestured for me to go on.

"The speaker of this poem wants to have sex," I explained.

"Whaatttt," Jason Burke drawled in disbelief.

"The speaker tells this woman that if they were both going to live forever, he'd take a lot of time and be romantic," I explained patiently. "But they're not, so he won't. He wants to have sex right away."

All through the room you could hear stifled laughter, a mild background sound, a buzzing, an indicator of excitement.

"All right, Mr. Frame," Mrs. Rove said.

She walked out in front of her desk and crossed her arms, like a challenge to me. She asked, "Can you back this theory up with some evidence from our poem here?"

I held the paper in front of my face and examined it critically, although I practically knew the thing by heart. "To His Coy Mistress" was in the seventeen-pound Norton poetry anthology I'd requested for my eighth birthday. I'd read it then, and after puberty I'd read the poem again and saw new meaning in it.

"The speaker asks for sex directly in the last paragraph. He says, 'let us sport us while we may.' Basically, 'let us do it.' And in the second stanza, he tries to scare her by saying that if they don't do it now, worms will get at her 'long preserved virginity.' The speaker thinks the girl has been a virgin for way too long.

"Further," I continued, "in the first stanza, the growing 'vegetable love' is actually the guy's erection."

All over the classroom, students sat straight up.

"Which," I added, grinning, "means the phrase 'vaster than empires' is pretty arrogant on his part."

Mrs. Rove removed her glasses. When she sat down behind her desk, she seemed to relinquish to me the run of the class.

"What about the title, Mr. Frame?" Mrs. Rove asked. "I'm sure you have something to say about that."

I cleared my throat, aware that everyone was watching me, and, for once, liking it.

"They said 'coy' back then," I said. "But today, we would call her...a cock-tease."

Nate Kirkland stopped midpick. Matt Katz had not only woken up, but started taking notes. Later I would see "get a vegetable boner" as that day's homework in his agenda. Jason Burke had surrendered to himself in the game of tic-tac-toe. And the girls in the class? The way the girls were looking at me, you would think that not only did I know what a pickle flip was, I could also do it damn well.

chapter

"I'm *not* going to Yeoman's party tonight," Jenny told me that Friday, hopping up on the hallway ledge where I was sitting, finishing my precalculus homework. For some reason, I always put off precalculus homework. Probably out of spite. I hate math—but don't tell Kate that.

I looked up. Jenny was wearing a skirt held together with safety pins. Were they fake, like the fruit bowls some people put on their tables? Or were they real safety pins? If I unhooked the safety pins, would her skirt fall open? Sometimes I had these involuntarily sexual thoughts about Jenny. Just because she's always around. And because I'm always having involuntary sexual thoughts.

"What party?" I asked.

"Will Yeoman's," Jenny said. "You know, Will Yeoman? That guy who's a dumber version of Jason Burke?"

"Oh, right," I said, graphing a squiggly parabola. Then I looked up at Jenny, amused. "He *is* a dumber Jason Burke."

Jason Burke was blond and good at sports and pretty smart. Will Yeoman was blond and good at sports, but a little rougher, a little bigger, and clumsier and stupider. Together they looked like a lesson on the evolution of man.

"Will Yeoman's parents are gone for the weekend," Jenny told me, pulling her legs up and crossing them on the narrow ledge. "So the party's in the whole house, not just the basement. Ashley Milano is gonna perform those stripper moves she learned from her pole-dancing lessons, and Will's creepy uncle is getting beer for the downstairs."

"That uncle who friended all those girls on Facebook?" I asked.

"Yeah."

"He'll probably try to come to the party," I said, remembering that was how else I had heard of Will Yeoman. Will Yeoman's uncle had "poked" Kayla Bateman on Facebook so much that she tried to get him on *To Catch a Predator*.

"Anyway, I'm not going." Jenny crossed her arms emphatically.

I scribbled "Finn Frame, Period Three Precalc" on my homework and closed my binder.

I asked Jenny what she wanted me to ask her: "Why aren't you going?"

The monologue that burst forth indicated that Jenny was very glad I had asked.

"It's just dumb girls who complain about how guys bother

123

them, but their complaints are *really* a thinly disguised boast of how much the guy likes them," Jenny began. "Like Kayla Bateman will talk about how senior guys throw food down her shirt when they're out to lunch, as if it's annoying, but the whole point of her bringing it up is to brag about how the senior guys take her out to lunch and that she has big boobs. I hate when all girls think about is guys."

This from a girl with a home library of heroines who donned stilettos and low-cut dresses while running to escape mortal danger. Ah, well.

"Is Will, like, inviting people to his party?" I asked.

This placated Jenny. She went on a whole rant about how Will never specifically invited her to his parties, but the Monday after his parties, he'd ask, "Hey, why didn't you show up, Jenny?"

"So I guess I'm supposed to, like, *assume* I'm invited," Jenny said. "Or he'll be mad that I didn't go!"

Jenny especially liked this idea, the idea that Will would be upset if she didn't show up to his party — or that he would notice. From what I'd seen at Pelham Public, people kind of forgot about Jenny. These kids had all known one another since they had baby teeth. They only found interesting those classmates who had undergone big changes since those days — for example, everyone was *very* interested in Kayla Bateman's big changes.

But even when she's super gothed out, Jenny doesn't stand out like that. Everyone at school has known her — quirky, small, and harmless—since kindergarten. When she wears shirts displaying firey tongues or knives dripping with blood, they just look down at her and say, "Hey, Jenny."

"Hey, Jenny," Jason Burke said, stopping by our ledge. "Can I borrow the precalc homework?"

"Yeah, sure! I'm just finishing it now," Jenny said. She has a poorly concealed crush on Jason Burke, although she always says, "Pelham boys are sooo dumb."

"Can I bring it to you in homeroom?"

"Great. Thanks so much, Jenny." And Jason took off at a jog.

Jenny turned to me. "Finn, can I have your homework?"

At lunch, Kate asked me, "Are you going to Yeoman's party tonight?"

"Yeoman's? How do you know about that?" I scoffed at her.

"Everyone knows about that," she said.

"You're a sophomore," I told her with disdain. "You're too young for underage drinking."

"Shut up!" Kate said, and she hit me lightly. My arm felt hot where she'd touched it. "I don't drink. And I don't really go to parties."

Wow! Kate was really brave to say that out loud! I was so impressed. There were at least ten kids in earshot of us, and Kate was admitting that she didn't drink. That was like me casually proclaiming I had an undescended testicle (I don't, I swear! I'm just saying it's considered freakish not to drink or go to parties when you're a high school student. No offense to the undescended).

No matter how much Johnny Frackas bugged me at St. Luke's, I hadn't ever admitted that I just didn't want to drink. I made up a football team's worth of imaginary drinking buddies to avoid this revelation. But Kate was just so *cool*. She could admit that she didn't like drinking or parties, and it didn't make her lame. It only made her...*cooler*.

"That's amazing!" I burst out.

She gave me a strange look.

"I mean, that's cool," I said. "That you don't go to parties. Parties aren't that...cool."

"I was *gonna* say," Kate continued, "if you're not going to Yeoman's, you should come see that new action movie with me. Apparently these agent guys have better suits than Will Smith in *Men in Black*."

"Oh, yeah," I said. I was smooth and casual, but in reality the idea of hanging out with Kate outside of school made me feel like I could hurdle Mount Everest. "That sounds...yeah, sure. Yeah."

"So you're not going?" Kate asked.

"What?"

"To Yeoman's."

"Nah. I was gonna skip it anyway."

"Good!" Kate said, twisting off her Snapple cap. "I haven't been to the movies in forever. Can you pick me up?"

"Yeah, sure," I said. "Does anyone else need a ride?"

"Like who else?"

"Who's coming?"

Kate shrugged. "You can invite whoever you want."

"No, but, who did you invite?"

"You."

"Just me?" My voice squeaked on "me," and I coughed elaborately to cover it up.

Kate raised an eyebrow. "Yes."

"So just you and me," I confirmed, trying to pitch my voice lower.

"Don't worry, it's not a girly movie or anything," she said. "There's lots of explosions and guy stuff for you."

Wow. Kate was not just asking me to a movie; she was asking me to a movie she'd chosen for a *guy*. So she thought of me as a *guy*. One who needed blood and action and superpowers. I'd always assumed if a girl took me to a movie, it would be Jane Austen's latest sappy big-screen resurrection. Okay, so that had already happened. And that "girl" had been my mom.

"I live in Larchmont," Kate continued. "Do you know how to get there?"

"Larchmont?" I said. "That's, like, four towns north of here, isn't it?"

She said, "Twenty minutes, tops. I'll buy the popcorn."

"Wait, aren't you in a different school district?" I asked.

Most Pelham Public kids lived, like I did, less than a mile from our school.

"I switched schools, but my parents didn't want to move," Kate said. "So I actually pay tuition here. Don't tell anyone; it's totally lame."

"Weird," I said. "Why did you switch?"

"Just geeky stuff," Kate said. "They didn't have as many AP math classes." She shrugged. "So I'll text you my address!"

Switching schools to take AP classes seemed weird to me, but the thought passed quickly through my very occupied brain. All my neurons were charged and chest-bumping each other with the joy of knowing that I, Finbar Frame, was going out with Kate.

That night, I was leaving the house at the same time as Luke, who was going with some teammates to the bars on Arthur Avenue. Arthur Avenue is in the Bronx, near Luke's school. I would have slaughtered Luke, Cain and Abel–style, for use of the Volvo on this particular night. Luckily, he didn't need the car because (a) he could take the train there and (b) going to a bar underage and then driving is five times dumber than just going to a bar underage. Which Luke was already doing.

"Do you have a fake ID?" I asked him as we both grabbed jackets from the closet near the front door.

"I just got one yesterday," Luke said. "This senior guy doctors up fake IDs in the bathroom at school."

Luke took out his wallet and showed me the ID card. It was an Alabama license, and the guy on it had a beard.

"No way are you this guy!" I laughed aloud, snatching the card from Luke's hand. "This guy's, what, forty? Oh my God, he was born in the seventies, he *is...*"

"Where's everyone going?" my mother asked.

She came out of the kitchen holding what looked like a cell phone. Luke and I knew it was actually a handheld UV light that killed germs. My mother regularly woke us up by shooting laser beams at the invisible bacteria around our room.

"Finn's taking the car to the movies," Luke said. "I'm going to a Fordham Prep thing."

"What kind of Fordham Prep thing?" my mother asked.

"Some school ministry thing," Luke said. "Prayers, refreshments, you know."

"I knew Fordham Prep would be good for you!" My mother clapped her UV light between her palms.

While she was kvelling over Luke's deepened Catholicism, I pushed open the door. I was glad my mother was focused on the bad twin. It allowed me to slip out with just a "Bye, Mom!" and avoid interrogation that would lead to a million questions about Kate.

Luke followed me down the front steps a few seconds later.

"Prayers?" I smirked, beeping the Volvo alarm off from a few feet away.

Luke crossed himself before heading off on foot to the train station. "I'll say grace before my first Bud Light. And I'll say a prayer for you, too, Finn — for your date."

Later that evening, after the movie, Kate and I left the theater side by side. As we emerged from the dark and I was blown away by how she looked in the renewed light, she asked me, "What'd you think?"

What did I think? I thought Kate fit perfectly in my passenger seat, asking politely before she scanned the radio on commercial. I thought she had great taste in music (she had turned off Nickelback and turned on the new Jay-Z song). I thought Kate had great taste in snacks (popcorn with extra artificial butter, orange Fanta), although I was tortured by the popcorn smell and wished vampires indulged, at least in Junior Mints, once in a while. I thought Kate had a laugh so great that every time she laughed, I wished I had written the script (although, actually, the scriptwriters hadn't meant the script to be funny. It was just funny because it was so bad). I was crazy about her.

"It was ridiculous to begin with," I said. "Then Miley Cyrus showed up!"

"I know, right?" Kate laughed. "I mean, is she really the first person the mayor of New York would call to fight terrorism?"

"Miley Cyrus shouldn't be allowed in action movies. Or *any* movies."

"Hey, hold up." Kate grinned. "You better make an exception for *Hannah Montana: The Movie.*"

"Ohhh," I said, nodding knowingly. "So you were a Hannah Montana girl?"

"So what?" Kate said defensively. "I bet you were a Pokémon guy. C'mon, admit it, you were a Pokémon guy."

"Not even close," I told her.

Mental note: hide three binders of Pokémon cards. Change eBay username from Pikachu4U. To...well, anything else.

As I drove Kate home, I was a little worried, because so far she had shot down any attempt of chivalry on my part. She'd opened the car door for herself, even though I tried to beat her to it. I'd let her step ahead of me in the ticket line, but then she'd been called down to the farthest ticket counter, and as I was trying to decide if I should follow her, I got called to the closest ticket counter. So she paid for her own ticket. All these things made me wonder if I could call this a date, or if it was just two people hanging out to avoid watching Ashley Milano strip-dance at a crowded kegger. Maybe I'd given Kate the "just friends" impression by not opening her car door or paying for her movie ticket. Or maybe I'd given her the "crappy date" impression.

Or maybe she was a militant feminist and my paying for her ticket or holding her door would have offended her. Yes, totally. My wussiness was a good thing.

But when we got a little closer, Kate began to fidget with the zipper of her jacket. And she actually sounded nervous when she spoke up over the Jay-Z song on the radio.

"Hey, Finn, I have a favor to ask."

A favor? I'm sure I could oblige. Did she need me to kiss

her? Lean over the gearshift and take off her shirt? Throw her in the back and . . .

"Can you come say hi to my dad?"

Wow. So the opposite of what I had in mind.

But I answered, "Sure," automatically.

Nerves shot through me and made it extra difficult to parallel park. I really needed to make a good impression on Kate's dad. He wanted to make sure that I was a safe and dependable guy. . . . Wait, hold up . . . this was fantastic! That meant that Kate had insinuated somehow that I was *not* a safe and dependable guy. How awesome! Kate didn't think I was safe and dependable (or rather, she didn't *know* I was safe and dependable). Kate thought I was dark and mysterious! She thought I was dangerous, which was miraculous, considering the whole night I'd stayed five miles below the speed limit. This whole vampire thing must be working!

Or maybe Kate's dad thought I was a different kind of dangerous. Maybe he thought I was someone way worse than a vampire. Maybe he thought I was an older guy who had a decent chance of scoring with his daughter. He thought this was a date. I practically skipped around the car to climb Kate's front steps. This *was* a date!

chapter

Something drew me again and again to the conflict between Chris Perez and Chris Cho. I shouldn't have cared. Not only was apathy part of my vampire agenda, but I had never spoken to Perez or Cho in my life. Yet I kept finding excuses to leave physics between the class period and the lab period. I even volunteered to be shot during the paintball lab so I could escape to my locker for a change of clothes. When I reached my locker, I would watch from twenty-five feet down the hall while Chris Perez robbed Chris Cho.

The first few times I watched, Perez roughed Cho around a little bit. He pulled at the lapels of his jacket to bring him close, then pushed him back into a locker or a bathroom door. He cuffed him on the jaw a little too hard. Then Perez would pat down Cho's chest and his jacket pockets. He'd undo the Velcro of Cho's pocket, dig inside, and pull something out. He treated everything as if it were his, violating Cho's Velcro, his jacket, his wallet.

Perez started by taking cash. Whatever Cho had on him. Cho wised up and started carrying less cash on him—down from two twenties, to a few singles, finally to no cash at all. But then Perez stole his leather wallet. After his wallet was gone, Cho would purposefully bring in objects, offerings for the ancient god that was Chris Perez. A CD or DVD, then this gold key ring that looked like it should have belonged to a mafioso, not a pubescent Asian American. Once I saw Cho try to give Perez a book. Perez rejected that, turned Cho's backpack upside down, flipped his pockets inside out, and took his iPod Touch instead.

A few weeks into school, Jenny had told me that Perez was a bullshitter and no one in his family was an immigrant. He was actually really rich. His father owned the biggest spring-break resort in Puerto Vallarta, and his mom was blond with fake boobs. She'd almost been chosen to be one of the housewives in *The Real Housewives of New York City*. The only true part of his sad tale was that his mother may or may not have been a stripper, but either way they'd never gone hungry.

So was I obsessing about Perez and Cho because Perez was a spoiled liar and a jerk to steal someone else's stuff when he was rich? Actually, that wasn't why. It wasn't even Perez's behavior that bothered me most. It wasn't how possessive he was, how he put his hands all over Cho in an odd, almost seductive manner. It wasn't the voice he used when he dug in

134

his pockets, this wheedling, creepy voice, like the one Harry Potter used when he talked to snakes. It wasn't the praise he heaped upon Cho when he'd given him what he wanted.

It was Cho's behavior that bothered me. You couldn't even call what Perez was doing "stealing" anymore. Cho was just handing all his crap over! That drove me crazy—how Cho shuffled down the hallway so dutifully, like Dilbert heading back to his cubicle. How he slumped his shoulders in that oversize jacket. How he didn't even walk down the other side of the hallway. How he didn't run. How he didn't raise his hands to shield his face. How he didn't push Perez away from his pockets. How he didn't protect himself. How he didn't even try some second-grade karate or order pepper spray off the Internet. How he didn't defend himself.

How much he was like me.

I watched the robbery go down at least once a week throughout September. But I kept a safe distance at first. Sure, Cho was acting like I had at St. Luke's—but he wasn't me, and I wasn't at St. Luke's anymore. I told myself I was not only far from Chris Cho, but far from the passive, bullied guy I myself had been, that guy who couldn't come up with an answer for Johnny Frackas. Now I was powerful. I had friends. I not only spoke up, I said "cock-tease" in English class. I told myself I should stop obsessing. But I kept obsessing. So, in October, when Perez took Cho's cell phone, I did something.

Cho had almost made it to his math class when Perez slammed open the door of the bathroom. He crossed the hall in three strong strides. Having left class, supposedly to retrieve my lab report, I was watching from my locker, three classroom doors down the hall.

"Chris Cho," Perez called loudly. "Buddy. BFF. What do you have for me today?"

Briefly, Cho raised his shoulders, then let them fall.

"You don't know?" Perez said. He bent down and got right in Cho's face, breathing on Cho's nose and mouth. "You want me to find out? You get off on this, Cho?"

Cho turned his head away from Perez's breath and said something I didn't hear.

"What was that?"

Perez hadn't heard either.

"I don't have anything today," Cho said.

"Cho, don't sell yourself short," Perez cajoled. He took an odd sort of encouraging tone with his victim. He was giving Cho a pump-up speech.

"You're loaded," Perez encouraged Cho. "You're a very lucky kid, ya know that?"

"I don't have anything today," Cho mumbled again.

But Perez knew Cho was lying. Perez had this built-in radar for valuables. He was like one of those scanners old people use to find coins at the beach. Sensing there was nothing worth robbing in Cho's backpack, Perez ripped it out of Cho's hand and sent it spinning across the hallway. It landed two feet in front of my locker, but neither of them looked back or noticed me. Then Perez pulled up Cho's jacket. Nothing worthwhile in there, either. Perez wrapped his hands around

Cho's hips and basically grabbed his ass. With one hand, he slowly pulled away his prize of the day.

Cho's cell phone was flat and sleek, silver with a touch screen and a full keyboard. It was a really nice phone. $350, easy. What did Perez do with these things? Sell them? Or use them himself, flaunting Cho's stuff in his face? And what did Cho do once they were taken? What would he do without his cell phone? What would he tell his parents had happened to it?

"Hey," I called down the hallway.

Cho looked more scared than Perez did. Neither of them had known I was there.

Perez looked back only briefly. The only effect I had on him was speeding up the process. He dangled Cho's phone in front of his eyes, let it slip from between his thumb and forefinger, and then dropped it in his own shirt pocket.

"Taxed!" Perez said merrily, and spun off to jog down the hallway.

Slowly and deliberately, I picked up Cho's backpack from the floor, walked over, and handed it to him. The whole time I was breathing heavily, preparing. Then with a manic change of speed, I took off after Perez.

When I sped up, he sped up. And even in enormous jeans with chains dragging them down and unlaced shoes, Chris Perez was fast. His pants slipped down his thighs as he ran. I got such a nice shot of his ass that I could've picked it out of a lineup. His sneaker soles squeaked in the empty hallway. But none of this slowed Perez down.

The incredible thing, though, was this: I was faster. This hallway, West Corridor, was long and clear and I pushed off the waxed tile floor, blood flooding my pumping arms and my long legs. Taking powerful strides, I cut across five floor tiles at a time. Everything was sharp and focused and working together: my hands and elbows in line, my heels kicking back behind me, my body propelling me forward faster than I could think or breathe. I know that I'm not a superhero. I know that I don't have special powers. But in that moment, I felt like I did.

Chris Perez was running on one side, along the lockers, and I was running on the other side, along the classroom doors. But I ran at an angle. I cut across. When I caught up, I caught up at Chris's left shoulder. I dug the palm of my right hand into his shoulder and turned him so he was facing me. Then, with both palms, I slammed him into the lockers.

As a child, when I caught up with Luke when he got lost, I'd always pull him back. I would grab him and pull him back toward me, toward home, toward safety.

But with Chris Perez, I pushed. I pushed him away from me and into the wall. The back of his skull cracked against the wooden beam above the lockers. The chains of his jeans clanged against one of the combination locks.

Perez was surprised I'd caught up so fast, but he was still quick and feisty. He shoved me off him, but I plunged immediately back, forcing my fists into his neck. To hold the rest of his body back, I raised my knee to pin his left hip into the lockers. With the fist not holding the cell phone, he swung at me, but my arms were longer than his and kept me at a safe enough distance. I was taller than Perez, too, by at least four inches, and I emphasized this by looking down on him.

"Drop Cho's phone," I ordered.

"Fuck you, Frame," he choked out hoarsely.

I was briefly flattered that he knew who I was. It actually gave me confidence.

"Feel dizzy?" I asked him. "I've got your jugular. And since you're a dumbass, I'll tell you what your jugular is. It's the thing that takes blood from your brain."

Thank you, Mr. Muncher. Our ninth-grade biology teacher at St. Luke's had taught us the location of the jugular vein, and also how to use the veins and arteries of the neck in a fight. My life was hell for three weeks after, as I was daily slammed against lockers while some jerk like Johnny Frackas dug his hands into my throat. I remembered the sensation, pinned up and back, trying to jerk forward but feeling first light-headed, then powerless as numbness tingled its way down my arms.…

Perez's fingers ungripped. I felt them go loose next to my knee. Cho's phone dropped next to Perez's wide-legged jeans.

Then Perez struggled suddenly, forcing his body forward. He was really strong, and he was kind of banging me around. No longer holding the phone, he had both hands free to grab at my arms, my hands. I made sure my body was far enough back that he couldn't get at my stomach. But I focused on keeping my hands on his neck.

"Give back his other shit, too," I said.

"Who gives a shit," Perez wheezed.

His instinct was to be a smartass. His reflex was to refuse. But then he shut up, and his face changed. His jaw slacked. His eyelids got heavy. He was feeling dizzy, I could tell. And scared—he was scared.

I had Chris Perez exactly where I wanted him. I felt adrenaline throbbing through me, heating my skin. I was focused and fearless. I was dangerous. I was powerful. I was bloodthirsty. This is the moment when my fangs would have come out. They didn't, but I was still full of conviction.

I was a vampire.

chapter

At home that night, assuming that chasing and choking a guy in the hallway would eventually elicit punishment, I decided to jump the gun and tell my parents.

"I kind of got into a fight today," I said at dinner.

It's hard to say that casually. Even though my voice was calm, my mom dropped a full bowl of salad. She had read an article on eating local, so she'd stolen a bunch of greens from our neighbor's garden.

"What happened?" she asked, frantically rushing over to examine me. "Where did he hit you? Do you have a concussion? You're not going to sleep tonight. Paul, keep him awake tonight."

"He didn't get your face, Finn," my dad said enthusiastically, inspecting me for black eyes. "That's the important thing. At least he didn't hit your face."

"He didn't hit me at all," I said.

"Did someone stop him?" my mother asked. "Did a teacher stop him?"

"*I* stopped him!" I yelled in frustration. Why did even my own parents assume I was a wuss? "*I* stopped *him. I* hit *him.*"

"Oh, Finbar," my mother moaned. She knelt helplessly among her purloined parsley. "You're a bully."

"He's a fighter!" my father boomed, suddenly loud and boastful. "Like his old man!"

Says the man who, as a college hockey player, performed a triple axel to avoid a confrontation on the ice.

"What'd you do to him?" Luke asked eagerly.

"He was being a jerk," I said. "He was picking on a freshman."

My mother pulled up greens off the floor with her tongs and put them on my plate.

"You're falling apart, Finbar!" my mother said. "You've changed. You're not even involved in anything anymore! Why aren't you writing for the paper or working on the literary magazine?"

"I might join this investment club," I volunteered.

"Greed," my mother asserted, shoving contaminated floor-salad in my face. "Greed and violence will get you nowhere, Finbar."

* * *

Pelham Public's principal, Dr. Hernandez, took two full days to call me into his office to talk about the fight. I had been kind of sweating it out the whole time. I knew that Dr. Hernandez knew about the "fight" because of the way it had ended. Mr. Pitt came out of his class when I was still cutting off the oxygen to Chris Perez's brain.

"Hey, what's going on here?" Mr. Pitt had asked.

I pulled back right away, but the whole thing looked suspicious. We were too close to each other. I was all guilty and flushed. Perez was panting to catch his breath, and his pants were around his knees. Actually, now that I think about it from Mr. Pitt's perspective, maybe it didn't look *The Outsiders* suspicious as much as it looked *Queer as Folk* suspicious. Probably our teacher didn't know what to think.

So, anyway, I was sweating out a punishment due to my cruel Catholic upbringing. At St. Luke's the teachers were completely sadistic. Detention consisted of standing six inches from the blackboard staring at a dot for thirty minutes without moving. If you looked away or even blinked for too long, you got ten extra minutes. Then there was the punishment called JUG—Judgment Under God. Basically, rebels were sent to sit on the school steps in the cold to wait for a lightning bolt to smite them for the horrible transgression of mismatched socks or passed gas during a prayer.

Pelham Public High School was completely different. There was no God to judge us here. Actually there were probably a bunch of deities floating around—one fiery pork-hating god for the Jews, and also for half Jews like Kayla Bateman; a mild WASP-y god with good manners for the Protestant kids in polo shirts. But our teachers weren't allowed to talk about any of them. Plus, there was that curious attitude of relaxation I had sensed the first day. I don't just mean all the napping. I'm talking about discipline.

For example, Pelham had a theater teacher who smoked cigarettes in the parking lot with students and told them about her messy divorce. When a cell phone rang during a lecture in my history class, the owner not only answered the phone but also held her finger up to the teacher and asked, "Can you keep it down for a second?"

And once, a sophomore English teacher, Mr. Watts, found out that one of his students had spent the past eight class periods carving an elaborate design into his desk. The "artwork" read: "Mr. Watts and Dickens sucks dick." Mr. Watts confronted the carver, telling him, "That's wrong!" Then Mr. Watts took the knife and crossed out the last *s* in *sucks*. "This sentence has two objects," he explained. "You need to conjugate the verb differently." And he handed the knife back.

Our principal was probably the source of all this relaxation. Not that he was exactly relaxed. More like confused. Dr. Hernandez stood in his doorway between classes and waved awkwardly to the students who rushed past, calling them by names that were not only incorrect but also bizarre. "Good afternoon, Jarvis," he would say to Jason Burke. Or "Aster," with a nod to Ashley.

So I wasn't surprised when Dr. Hernandez addressed me

as "Phineas" when he emerged from his office to find me in the waiting room, biting my nails while sitting between his two secretaries. After he pulled his office door shut behind me, he asked, "It *is* Phineas, isn't it?"

"Close enough," I said as we each took a seat.

I'd never been called into the principal's office in my life. It was a little different than I'd expected. The secretary had seemed confused and a little bit annoyed by me, and when Dr. Hernandez led me inside, he offered me five different things — coffee, tea, water, soda, and breath mints (was that a hint?) — before he sat down.

"Well, Phineas," he began sadly.

I was already contemplating possible punishments. I could deal with detention, which consisted of pushing a large trash can around to different classrooms and emptying smaller trash cans into it. I could even deal with the orange juvie-looking vest they made you wear for trash duty. I wouldn't be thrilled, though, if my punishment lowered my GPA. Somehow, though, I didn't get the sense that Dr. Hernandez even had the power to change my GPA.

"This sort of behavior," he began. "Running in the hallways. Slamming people into lockers. Threatening people."

"Yes."

Dr. Hernandez shook his head.

In imitation, I shook my head.

"I see that you agree," Dr. Hernandez said, setting his hands flat on his desk.

"I agree, sir," I said.

All he had done was list my behaviors. He hadn't condemned them. Yes, I had run in the hallway, slammed Perez into a locker, and threatened him. I agreed completely.

"And if you had to come in here again..." Dr. Hernandez began. A phlegmy cough seemed sufficient to complete his threat. If I had to come in here again, Dr. Hernandez would cough on me. After the cough, he looked up at me expectantly.

"Completely fair," I said.

Looking around the room at Dr. Hernandez's framed pictures, in which he was shaking hands with administrators, local politicians, and Pelham Public valedictorians and athletes, I noticed a consistent theme. The poor man always seemed a little lost. The expression on his face said, "What is that big light you're flashing at me, and who is this person again?" Poor confounded principal. My father had much the same face in many of our family photo albums — why were my supposed male role models so bewildered?

Now Dr. Hernandez stood up and extended his hand.

"It seems that we understand each other, Phineas," he told me.

"I think we do, Dr. Fernandez," I concurred.

"Huh?"

By the time he realized my mistake, I had my backpack on and was headed for the doorway. I didn't blame Dr. Hernandez for his lack of disciplinary action. If I'm going to give him credit, I might say that he knew that I was a good kid and Chris Perez was a bad kid who had gotten away with too much already. Maybe this was kind of a "thank you."

* * *

What about Chris Perez? You may expect, as my nervous stomach expected, that he would pay me back with a beatdown.

Chris Perez could have issued to his many followers and admirers throughout the school a death warrant for me. He could have made it hell for me to turn any corner. He could have run me over (Chris Perez was only fifteen, but somehow he had a driver's license. Chris Perez got everything he wanted). He could have reduced me to a skinny speed bump in the school parking lot. And yet, he did nothing.

Okay, he did some things. He muttered things under his breath, things like:

"Your dick must be small to fit up Cho's ass."

But I would just stare at him. Like I was waiting. Like he must have some better insult than that.

Perez would look away; he didn't like me staring at him. He said it was because I was gay, but I think he was sort of scared. The last time I had stared at him, he'd lost the ability to breathe. He'd started to go numb. Maybe he'd believed, for a split second, imprisoned in my merciless, creepy see-through eyes, that he would die.

Now I was pretty sure he thought I was a psycho. The type of kid who, if you pushed him over the edge, would show up to school in a trench coat with the pockets full of knives. Not the most flattering perception, but it kept him away from me.

147

As for everyone else, this isolated incident of violence helped my reputation tremendously. Apparently, shortly after "the fight," Kayla Bateman was telling stories about me to people in study hall. Jenny confronted her, claiming that *she* knew more about me than anyone else, and if anyone should be telling Finbar stories, it should be Jenny. Anyway, Jenny and Kayla already didn't get along because of the dichotomy in their bra sizes, and they got into a fight trying to prove they knew me better. This alone is proof of how ridiculous Kayla is, because I've had one conversation with her in my life, and it went: "Can I borrow a pen?" "No. My other one exploded." But anyway, somewhere during the Fight for Finbar, laying down the trump card of Finbar knowledge, Jenny revealed to Kayla that I was a vampire.

So one day in mid-October, at the lockers only a few feet down from mine, Ashley Milano was going on and on about how I couldn't have really caught Chris Perez in the hallway, couldn't have really pinned him against the locker, couldn't have choked him without getting my ass kicked.

"And Finbar doesn't have any bruises or a black eye or *anything*," Ashley Milano said. "And we would see if he did, because he's really pale."

"He's pale for a reason," Kayla whispered ominously, her voice carrying over her own breasts.

Ashley ignored that. "And Finbar would never win. Chris Perez skips, like, three classes a day to go to the fitness center. He's in crazy good shape."

"But I've heard Finbar's, like... *freakishly* strong," Kayla said.

They both looked over at me in wonder. I happened to be having trouble getting my locker open, which was ironic. When I did finally open it, I did it with a flourish and then kind of flexed. Awkwardly, of course.

"Finbar's really tall," Ashley admitted. "But his muscles don't look that big."

"But he's got these crazy reflexes," Kayla continued. "Finbar can *sense danger.*"

"How do you mean?"

Kayla fished a pack of Tic Tacs out of her cleavage and shook a few into Ashley's hand before continuing her explanation.

"It's like *Twilight*," Kayla said. "You know how Edward stops the car just before it hits Bella in the parking lot? Finbar is like *that.*"

Kayla winked a bunch of times.

"Is there something wrong with your mascara?" Ashley asked.

"No," Kayla said pointedly. "I mean, Finbar is like *that.*"

Ashley gasped. "Like..." She leaned over to whisper something into Kayla's ear. Kayla nodded vigorously and both of them shrieked. Then they turned to look at me.

At that exact moment, I happened to be unwrapping a stick of Doublemint. I folded it nonchalantly into my mouth. Then I threw the wrapper on the ground, littering carelessly.

"He's so cool," Ashley sighed.

* * *

The second most unexpected reaction to my actions came about a week afterward, when I was leaving my Latin classroom. It was senior lunch period, and the hallways were crowded and noisy with people fighting over who got to drive and if they still wanted to go to Burger King now that the menu listed how many calories were in everything.

"Yo, Frame!"

I heard this call amidst all the brouhaha but continued down the hallway completely undisturbed. I didn't respond to *Frame*. Frame is a football player's name, a name that's shouted in locker rooms and across fields. Frame is a name for rooms full of sweaty men. My brother, Luke, was Frame. So I didn't turn around.

Then, I realized that Luke, owner and dominator of the name Frame, was ten miles south in the Bronx. I was Frame.

Pelham Public's assistant sports director, this guy Coach Doakes, who has taken self-tanning way too far, was hurrying his pumpkin-colored self after me down the hall. I swear to you I thought he was gonna track me down and chew me out for pussying out of gym and taking Nutritional Science instead. I was preparing an argument on how much I'd improved my quality of life by learning about the acai berry.

"Frame," Coach Doakes said seriously. "Word is you're a hell of a runner."

"Huh?"

150

Word? What word? Oh, probably the words of every kid who'd heard that poetry scholar Finbar Frame had somehow scared the shit out of Chris Perez.

"I'd love to see you run," Coach Doakes told me.

I looked at him, panicked. I thought he meant right then. I looked ahead of me and estimated how many freshman girls in ponytails I'd have to mow down to prove my athletic worth.

"What?"

"Tryouts for the track team are in ten days," Coach Doakes said. "I've already got a lot of sprinters. Muscle guys. What I need is endurance. Long-distance guys. Long, lean guys like you. With a frame like Frame. Ha! Get it?"

"Yeah." I gave him a queasy laugh.

"So you wanna run track?"

A vision of myself as the baby daddy from *Juno*, all short-shorts and bony shoulders, bounced disturbingly through my head. Any extracurricular that required tighty-whities made me wary. Then another thought made me wary. The sun. I imagined my pale exposed flesh baking and sweating in the sun for three hours every afternoon. I couldn't be out in the sun for that long. If I were, people would start to notice that I wasn't sparkling like Edward in *Twilight* or bursting into flames like Chauncey Castle from *Bloodthirsty*. They would know that I wasn't a vampire. Oh, and I'd break out into hives. That too.

"I'm not really…great…with the sun," I told Coach Doakes.

The coach didn't look at me like I was crazy, which most

people did when I talked about the sun like it and I were in a rocky romantic relationship.

"Frame, I'm talking winter track," Coach said impatiently. "*Indoor* track."

"Oh, psh," I breathed out, relieved. "Sure. Great."

"Great!" He clapped me on the back. "See ya at tryouts!"

Wait, what? I was so excited at avoiding the sun that I joined a varsity sport? I didn't even recognize myself anymore. And I wasn't even wearing the short-shorts yet.

The best reaction to my violence, though, was not my ambush varsity recruitment. The best reaction came the day after the fight happened. I still had some sore hamstrings from that unexpected hallway sprint (a sad comment on my physical fitness — and on Luke's ability as a personal trainer), so I was squatting and wincing as I dropped books onto the bottom of my locker before lunch.

"Hey, Tony Soprano," someone said.

I looked up and, despite my pain, smiled. It was Kate.

"What's that?" I asked Kate.

She was hanging on the open door of my locker, and I stood up quickly so it wouldn't look like I was looking up at her boobs. Which I had been, but only briefly and respectfully. Ouch, hamstrings.

"I hear you're kicking ass around here," Kate said. "Should I be scared?" She drew away from me, pretending to tremble. "I wouldn't want to provoke your rage."

"No rage here." I held my hands up in surrender.

I didn't want Kate to think of me as Chris Perez did—mentally unstable. That wasn't attractive.

"I just think Chris Perez is a jerk," I explained, shrugging.

"Me too," Kate said. "In chem class the other day, he spilled hydroxylic acid on me."

"Were you okay?" I asked. "Did it burn you or something?"

"Hydroxylic acid is water," Kate said, grinning.

Oh. Dumb Finbar. How did I get that A in chem last year?

"But he got my jeans wet," Kate continued. "And I had to borrow a pair of shorts from Audrey Li."

Audrey Li was a famed sophomore slut. "Oh, so you have scabies now?" I asked.

Kate laughed. "Pretty much," she said.

She stared at me for a second. Then she poked me in the shoulder.

"Does this provoke your rage?" she asked.

Her index finger poked my pale skin repeatedly, ranging from my shoulder to my collarbone. She asked repeatedly, purposefully annoying: "Does this provoke your rage? Does this provoke your rage? Am I provoking your rage?"

I was not provoked. I just stood there, laughing, calm, as people passed the open lockers, went through their lockers, trudged by in backpacks, turned into classrooms, walked out the doors. And in the midst of all this normalcy, I leaned

153

toward Kate, shaking my head, and then an extraordinary thing happened.

Kate had been poking the back of my neck, but then she used her fingers to pull me forward. There was no ambiguity about what she was doing, no question, none of the hesitation that characterized my whole life, and especially my love life.

Kate kissed me.

My first thought was, *She's giving me CPR!* That's how little sexual experience I have. Then I realized that I was *not* having a heart attack. This girl was voluntarily pressing her lips to mine. And she wasn't even trying to hide the kiss. People were watching—out of my peripheral vision, I saw half of Mrs. Anderson's fan club walk by. A whole bunch of guys were seeing me, Finbar, making out like a pimp.

After all these things ran through my head, I realized I had to kiss back.

I had barely lowered my lip to below hers when she pulled away. But I really don't think she pulled away out of repulsion. I'm pretty sure that was the natural ending to the kiss.... Right?

"Let's go to lunch," Kate said, like she kissed guys every day during fourth period by the lockers, and then went to eat chicken patties. Like this was normal. Instead of what it was to me, which was...incredible.

chapter

So you may ask, "Hey, Finbar, what's up with you and the sun? Do you still have a beef?" (Yeah, I'm now allowed to use "beef" when not referring to hamburgers. I beat up Chris Perez! I have street cred.)

Well, the answer is: I cannot defeat the sun. I can defeat Chris Perez, but I cannot defeat the sun. My first few days at Pelham Public I hiked from my crappy parking spot to my first period class. During those ten minutes outside, I didn't shrivel up and die or anything. But I did get a little itchy. And I didn't want to be known as that Itchy Kid. I'd be classified in the Untouchables along with Nate Kirkland.

So I retrieved my eighty-year-old-man sunglasses from the doctor and wore them to school every morning. I also wore this big sweatshirt that I stole from Luke and pulled the hood up over my head. Because of my whole incognito look, those skater kids who drew on their shoes mocked me every morning. They always sat on top of cars in the parking lot. They were always there, no matter how early I arrived. For guys who skipped every class, they were ridiculously punctual.

"Hey, it's the international man of mystery!" they'd call out to me.

Or "Hey, Mr. Hollywood!"

I would just duck my head and wave, as if I were in Hollywood and they were nonthreatening papparazzi.

By staying inside during lunch and slouching in the darkest, creepiest corners of all my classes (which was pretty vampiric anyway), I avoided any itching incidents. Before I realized it, I fell into a routine. And soon it was late October and cold enough that I actually needed my sweatshirt.

One morning Matt Katz told me, "I love this, man. When the weather gets cold."

He gestured outside, to the lovely autumn trees dropping dark red leaves on Mrs. Rove's Escalade. *Wow,* I thought. *Matt Katz is deeper than I thought. He really sees the beauty in nature. And all kinds of nature, not just that one type of grass...*

"Yeah," Matt Katz continued. "I get to wear my jacket with the big pockets!"

He flipped his jacket open to reveal two large pockets on the inside. Besides all the contraband he had stashed in there, which I won't mention for legal reasons, he also had two different iPod Nanos and a bunch of Werther's Original hard candies.

It was also in October that we realized that our physics teacher, who looked like Albert Einstein if he were a drag queen, was too busy crashing toy cars into the walls and measuring their velocities to notice if we showed up to our lab period. One day Jason Burke, Ashley Milano, and Jenny decided to take advantage of this by going to Dunkin' Donuts (or, as Ashley had dubbed it, Double D) third period instead of drawing vectors for forty-five minutes.

"Hey, Finn," Jason called to me on my way to the physics room. He jangled his car keys at me. "Come to Double D with us. Blow off lab."

I kind of froze in my tracks. This was a dilemma. On one hand, I had worked hard to establish myself as a guy who, as my admirers would say, "didn't give a shit." The badass Finbar who schooled Mrs. Rove about poetic erections wouldn't care if he got in trouble for skipping physics lab.

On the other hand, it was really sunny out today. The kind of sun that would make me break out like a biblical leper. I kind of gave a shit about that.

"Uh, nah, man," I told Jason. "I'm good, thanks."

"Come on," Jason said. "You can't get in trouble. You choked a guy and Dr. Hernandez just, like, asked you on a gay date."

"He didn't ask me on a gay date!" I said.

"Did he take you into his office alone?" Jason asked.

"Well, yeah, but…"

"Did he offer you candy?" Jason continued.

"Just a breath mint," I said.

"Aha!" Jason said. "The plot thickens."

Jason and I had kind of become friends. We started off teaming up on projects in physics lab (until he started cutting

157

class), but then he started telling me more personal things. Like how he was hooking up with both Kayla Bateman and Ashley Milano. Not both of them at the same time, though that would have been a much better story. Like a *Playboy* story. But he just took turns hooking up with them. First Kayla for a few weeks, then Ashley for a few weeks. According to Jason, each girl had both pros and cons. Kayla had...well, two *large* pros...but aside from that, she was apparently "kind of a snore," i.e., she wouldn't let Jason do anything more than kiss her. Ashley could get pretty wild. They'd hooked up in all these weird places around school, like the bullpen of the baseball field and the photography darkroom.

"How do you pull it off? Hooking up with two girls?" I asked him once, genuinely impressed. Kayla and Ashley were both pretty good-looking. Plus, they were friends with each other. Wouldn't they notice they were sharing Jason?

"Well, here's the secret," Jason told me. "Sometimes I just suddenly stop hooking up with both of them. Then they get mad, and they join forces against me. That keeps their friendship going."

Wow. Jenny had been right when she told me Jason was smarter than he looked.

Now it was tough to avoid his invitation to cut class, and he and Ashley were waiting for me to come with them. Jenny was waiting, too—waiting to see how I would get out of this. She knew it was too sunny out, and I think she almost wanted me to blurt out my secret to prove she knew more about me than anyone.

"Um," I said. "Well. Actually. I have this thing where...I can't go outside when it's really sunny."

"What?" Jason asked. "Like, when there's an eclipse?"

"No, like, a regular day," I said. "Like today. It's like...my skin...reacts badly. To sun."

Ashley Milano gasped. Actually, it was kind of a combo squeak-gasp. The noise conveyed so much astonishment that I *knew*. I knew that Jenny had told Ashley I was a vampire.

Just in case I wasn't sure, Jenny whispered pretty obviously to Ashley, "I told you so."

Jason didn't notice all the vampire gossip. Instead, he suggested, "I think Finn just wants to stay and hang with Kate."

Maybe Kate and I were big news around school. Maybe everyone was talking about us and speculating about our relationship. I had noticed some people smiling when they saw us together twice in one day, but most of the sophomores who saw us eat lunch together seemed to assume that because we were both new to Pelham, we knew each other from somewhere else. I wanted juniors to be talking about us, smiling at us, too. "Did you hear about Finn and Kate?" That was what I wanted, even more than everyone talking about me as a vampire. That was *why* I wanted everyone talking about me as a vampire: I wanted a girl.

"Right, sophomore Kate!" Ashley said. "She totally likes you, Finn! I read it in the gossip column."

"We have a school gossip column?" I asked.

I'd read the school newspaper a few times, mostly to criticize it and thus appease Jenny, whose pieces always got rejected by the douche bag editor. I'd never seen a gossip column. There was a perverted "guess the body part" photo display that constituted the Science Section, but apparently a gossip column would have been inappropriate.

"The gossip column is self-published," Ashley said with dignity.

"By *your* self," Jenny scoffed.

"On the girls' bathroom wall," Jason added.

"How'd you know that?" I began to ask Jason. Then I saw him and Ashley exchange guilty looks and stopped pursuing that subject.

"And, like, nothing in your gossip column is true," Jenny said pointedly, crossing her arms.

"Let's go," Jason said, tossing his car keys in the air and snatching them with one hand. "Finn — enjoy Kate." He added in a low voice as he passed me, "I recommend the third stall in the girls' bathroom."

In physics lab, I had to do a whole lot of vectors by myself. And while "vectors" sound like something that superheroes would shoot out of their eyes, they aren't as cool as they sound. They're really just arrows you draw on paper. I didn't care, though. I was in a great mood because everyone knew that Kate and I liked each other. Which meant that it was true that Kate liked me and not just something I'd created in my desperate mind.

It only takes a small dose of self-confidence to get me high on it, because I'm not used to having any. And I was drunk as hell on self-esteem when I met Kate at her locker for lunch.

"*Lolita!*" I greeted Kate's latest book.

As part of her quest to read classic novels, Kate had picked up *Lolita*, by Vladimir Nabokov.

"A classic and timeless story of an old pervert," I pronounced like a college professor.

Kate laughed, then said, "I'm actually having trouble getting through it."

"Creeped out?" I asked her.

Kate put *Lolita*, whose cover had a really inappropriate picture of some little girl's plaid skirt and bare knees, back in her locker.

"Nah." Kate shrugged. She smiled up at me. "I like older men."

Oh. Wow. She liked me. She completely liked me! I, Finbar Frame, was a stud. Even if the cafeteria was serving its suspiciously ambiguous "pasta casserole" for lunch, today was a great day.

Just then, I noticed for the first time a picture in Kate's locker. It was of a girl with super-long hair. She actually looked a lot like Kate. For a wild second I thought Kate had a twin sister too. Not only was she smart and gorgeous and quick on her feet—Kate was a twin, like me! Even stranger, like me, Kate had a twin who was the complete opposite of her. The girl in the locker picture was wearing a really short skirt and high heels. She had her tongue stuck out and looked drunk. Nothing like the cool, collected Kate.

"Is that your sister?" I asked, pointing to the picture.

"Oh." Kate looked up quickly. "Uh…that's a friend from my old school."

161

She slammed her locker quickly and seemed flustered. I shrugged it off and followed Kate to the cafeteria.

At lunch, something strange but kind of awesome happened.

Well, first, one of the skater kids came up to me in the lunch line as I was selecting a Snapple and said, "Hey-ooo, it's LC from *The Hills.*"

"I don't even have my sunglasses on," I told him.

"Whatever, dude," the skater scoffed.

Kate, ahead of me, scooped some spaghetti and meatballs onto her plate.

"What was that about?" she asked, nodding at the skater.

Oh, right. I'd told Kate I couldn't be out in the sun, but I'd tried to make it sound as manly as I could. Like I'd spent so many hours rock climbing with my raw muscles exposed and climbed so close to the sun that even my alligator-tough flesh had had all it could take. To keep this impression up, I'd avoided Kate whenever I was wearing my Hollywood shades.

"Those guys just like my sunglasses," I told Kate.

"What sunglasses?" she asked.

Never mind.

Okay, this wasn't the awesome thing that happened. The awesome thing happened after Kate and I sat down with our spaghetti. The awesome thing was that these two freshman girls came over to our table.

"Hey, Finbar." The girls giggled in unison.

"Um…"

How did these girls know my name? I'd never seen them

before. And they had really, really tight pants on. Not that that's relevant, but how did girls find such tight pants?

Anyway, simultaneously, each girl extended a piece of garlic bread.

"You want some garlic bread, Finbar?" they asked.

Just to set the scene, they each said this in the same way one would ask, "You want some help with those pants, sexy?"

I looked to Kate and shrugged. Although she looked amused, I reassured myself that she was concealing her jealousy by taking a bite of meatball. Or maybe she knew I'd never go for a girl in pants that tight.

"Garlic bread?" I repeated dumbly.

"Yeah," one girl said. "Nice and *garlicky*."

"Oh. Uh…no thanks," I told her.

She thrust the bread right against my face. I jerked my head back.

"You sure?" she asked.

"Yeah," I said. "Thanks, though."

I was completely puzzled until I heard the freshman girls' conversation as they walked away.

"He was totally scared of the garlic!" one squealed in delight.

"He *so* is what they said he is!"

A vampire! I *so* was a vampire! I swirled my spaghetti around my school-safe spork in triumph. Jenny knew I was a vampire and told Kayla Bateman. Kayla Bateman knew I was a vampire and told Ashley Milano. Ashley Milano knew I was a vampire and had probably published it on the bathroom wall. Now even freshman girls knew I was a vampire.

I looked over at Kate, who was calmly sipping her Snapple Green Tea like she was in some damn zen garden. As if she wasn't sitting across from a spine-chilling, bloodthirsty beast who got her heart pumping in more ways than one. Kate did not know I was a vampire. She hadn't even *heard* I was a vampire. Why didn't Kate gossip? More importantly, why didn't Kate ever use the third stall in the girls' bathroom?

The meatball on my plate put a new thought in my head. Maybe because I ate human food in front of Kate every day, she didn't believe I subsisted on the blood of unwilling victims. Damn lunch. Damn pasta casserole! Damn Hebrew National hot dog day. Damn my humanity!

"I think those girls have a crush on you," Kate observed calmly.

"I don't know," I said pointedly, swirling spaghetti around my plastic fork. "I wouldn't give GARLIC to someone I had a crush on. It almost seemed like they wanted to see how I reacted to GARLIC. Like, as if I were someone who had a thing about GARLIC."

Shrugging cluelessly, Kate didn't seem the least bit scared of me.

When I walked back to my locker with Kate, Jenny was waiting. She looked a little pissed off, and I wondered if Ashley Milano had spent their entire third-period trip to Double D lecturing Jenny about how many calories were in whipped cream.

"Do you have lunch with Kate, like, every day?" Jenny asked me when Kate had left.

"Yeah, basically," I said.

"But you don't see her *outside* of school, do you?" Jenny probed.

"Sometimes," I said. "Hey, are we still reading that geisha book in English?"

"You know, she wears her sweatpants over her jeans," Jenny told me.

"The geisha?" I asked, puzzled. "I thought they wore those red—"

"No!" Jenny said impatiently. "Kate. I'm in Ultimate Dodgeball gym class with her, and she doesn't actually change her clothes. She just puts on sweatpants over her jeans."

"Oh," I said. "Okay."

"Which probably means she's, like, really *sweaty*," Jenny told me. "Kate's probably really sweaty and gross."

I closed my locker and swung my backpack up onto my shoulder.

"I don't think so," I said.

As we walked down the hall, Jenny said, without looking at me, "I don't think she'd understand you."

"What?" I looked down at Jenny.

"You know." Jenny gestured to my face, then put both her index fingers up against her lips and turned them down. Fangs. Or walrus.

"I don't think she'd understand *what you are*."

Oh, right. I was a vampire. Well, I wasn't worried about Kate understanding that. I was busy hoping she would find out! So I just shrugged at Jenny.

"Besides," Jenny added huffily, looking away again, "Kate's, like, four pounds too heavy for her jeans. So it's good she covers them up with sweatpants."

As I followed Jenny into class, I thought about her weird obsession with people's jeans. She was always telling me if other girls were too big or too small for their jeans. And the weirdest thing was, she knew how big or how small by the *pound*. Kayla Bateman was six and a half pounds too big for her jeans, according to Jenny. How the eff did she know that? As for Jenny, she had to order these special jeans from Japan that were made for flat-assed Asian girls. Yeah, I'd heard all about it.

As Jenny pouted into her folders and binders, which were all *Eragon*-themed, I felt bad for her. As unmanly as I may be, sometimes I'm glad I'm a guy. It means I never have to get that bummed out by other people's jeans.

It was the night after Halloween, which I'd celebrated quietly by seeing a horror movie with Jenny, telling her, "I don't understand the big fuss about all this scary stuff, about fangs and monsters," and also by texting Kate while she gave out candy with her parents and by avoiding Ashley Milano's reality TV costume party.

166

At the dinner table, my mother announced to our family, "Luke is failing math."

Luke had about half a burger jammed in his mouth but managed to express himself by rolling his eyes.

"What's this?" my father asked, oblivious as usual.

"I went into school to speak with Luke's teacher today," my mother said. "His average is a fifty-six."

"What's that out of?" my father asked.

It's pretty obvious my dad had gotten into Boston College only because he was a varsity athlete.

"I hate proofs!" Luke finally swallowed and spoke. "They're so dumb. I shouldn't have to write a paragraph in math. The only good thing about math is I don't have to write stuff."

"If he doesn't bring his average up to a C," my mother said, "he can't play basketball this winter."

My father gasped. My mother had such huge tears in her eyes you would have thought Lysol had been discontinued. This was a monumental problem. Where else could Luke use his talents for knocking people over and running really fast and breaking guys' noses and making it look like an accident? If Luke couldn't play sports anymore, his only choice would be to join the Mafia.

"What math class are you in?" I asked Luke.

"I'm in Math B," Luke said.

"Finbar, could you work with him?" my mother asked, leaning into me. She gripped my arm like she was Leonardo DiCaprio and I was a lifeboat.

"I didn't take Math B," I said.

"What about the kids in your class?" she asked.

I thought about my precalculus class. I guess most of those Pelham Public kids had taken Math B last year. But currently, we were all pretty lost in math. Matt Katz was probably the smartest, but he was too busy resurrecting Tupac to help Luke. In terms of people who I wouldn't feel awkward asking to my house to tutor my brother, I knew Jenny best, but she was only pulling off a C through the mutual efforts of me and her statistician father.

Of course, there was Kate. She loved math. And she was taking Math B right now, so she would be doing exactly what Luke was. In fact, she would be such a perfect math tutor for Luke that I felt guilty for not suggesting her. But I wasn't ready for Kate to meet my family. I was almost as worried that my mom would scare Kate away as I was that my handsome brother would attract her back.

My dad turned to Luke and said, "You've just got to focus...."

Luke swallowed his last French fry and jumped up to scrape his plate above the garbage. He began humming loudly to drown out the conversation. I believe it was an R. Kelly song.

"Paul, it's harder for him," my mother said quietly.

Luke hummed louder, like screaming with his lips pursed. Yup, he was definitely humming "Trapped in the Closet."

"Well, maybe we should look into a new medicine."

"No!" Luke slammed his plate onto the dish rack next to the sink so hard it bounced back up.

"Luke, the plate!" From my mother.

Luke caught the plate and spun around. "I hate that medicine stuff."

"Sweetheart…" My mother's voice was calm, trying to soothe him — and preserve the wedding china that had somehow survived her wild son's childhood.

"I'm not fucking with my heart again," Luke said. "Then I won't be able to play sports at all. Just — let me deal with it."

"Luke —" my mother attempted.

"No!"

My mother's worst nightmare came true: Luke threw the plate on the ground. Unfortunately it didn't shatter into a million tiny pieces, which would have been much more exciting to watch. Instead, it sort of cracked, and the top part tipped over and clanked against our kitchen tile. Don't get me wrong, my mother still began to sob, but it wasn't as cool to watch.

Luke stormed upstairs and I watched in amazement. Usually he was pounding up those steps soaked in pheromone-filled sweat and exercise endorphins, singing a Rihanna song at the top of his lungs. Luke hadn't always been an easy kid to raise, but he had always been a happy one. While I was often moody and irritated and prone to shutting myself in my closet, displaying many signs of a future serial killer, Luke was always moving, smiling, always happy, always busy. But of course Luke was happy, I'd always thought. He was good at sports, girls liked him, and he had a hell of a tan. What was not to be happy about? Now for the first time, I wondered if Luke was actually happy because he *decided* to be happy. I wondered this because for the first time I realized that between his grades, his failed medications, and his frustration at not being able to sit still—it might not always be easy to be my brother.

chapter

The first Monday in November, none of us skipped physics lab. But many of us would later wish we had.

Our teacher, Einstein in Drag (henceforth called Einstein for short), had gotten us all excited about this particular lab. It was a competition among two-person teams to see who could build the best roller coaster out of these plastic toy pieces. Once you built it, you had to race toy cars along the track. What, you may ask, made it the "best" roller coaster? Basically, you got lots of points for each fancy-schmancy addition: a really high peak, a really sharp turn, and, the king of all kings, the loop-de-loop. Oh, and you lost a hell of a lot of points if your car went off the tracks, because that meant that your riders died. However, you didn't lose *all* your points, which showed how sadistic our teacher was.

And let me tell you — when you're making a roller coaster, it's damn hard not to kill people. In fact, I'm scared to ride a roller coaster ever again. Jason Burke and I were complete failures at the really sharp turn and the loop-de-loop. The really sharp turn threw our car violently across the room each time, and the loop-de-loop resulted in our car just dropping straight down to the ground. So we decided to focus on one high peak and named our coaster Everest. We decided our ride would be all about marketing.

Unfortunately, we couldn't even master that one high peak. Every time it approached, the car would roll backward. But at least no one died.

At the lab table next to ours, Matt Katz was building an epic roller coaster called the Ball Screamer. The name was weird, but the roller coaster's motto was simple: "You'll scream your balls off." On Matt Katz's team, Matt was the visionary, and Kayla Bateman, his partner, did all the dirty work. First, Kayla had to count out all the pieces they needed to build Matt's scrawled-blueprint masterpiece. Then, after she'd discovered they were forty pieces short, Kayla had to steal pieces from other groups. We were each only supposed to have fifty. I let Kayla have five of ours. She could be persuasive somehow.

"All right!" Einstein waved to us from the front of the classroom. "By now, your coaster should be working. And you should have recorded the average velocity of your car."

I frowned at Jason. He shrugged.

"I'll be watching for cars going off the tracks," Einstein continued. "It's go time!"

Matt Katz directed Kayla. "Get at the end of the coaster to catch the car."

"Get them in place now. And when I blow the whistle...GO!"

Jason fumbled with our car at the start of our track. Everest built momentum on a series of small hills. "Go!" Jason and I cheered urgently, guiding the car with our eyes like it was a bowling ball. "Keep going! Faster!"

The car directly disobeyed us. It barely attempted the big hill before stalling and falling lazily backward, like an old man sinking into his couch.

Jason groaned. "Do you think we'll fail?" he asked.

I shrugged. "We didn't kill anyone."

We turned to watch the Ball Screamer, which was still going because it was extra long from all the stolen pieces. Matt was watching it like a crazy person, his face bright red, his fist clenched.

"Yes!" he'd cry out each time it made a turn. "Yes!" When it made it over a hill, Matt Katz got so loud that the whole class turned to look. And Einstein was loving it. She watched in wonder as the Ball Screamer looped its loop—and didn't drop!

"An A, Mr. Katz!" Drag Einstein proclaimed.

Matt Katz was thrilled. He was so thrilled, in fact, that he forgot about Kayla, who was still waiting at the end of the roller coaster. Kayla was only mildly interested in the loop-de-loop, and she didn't watch it carefully enough to realize that the car had really gained a lot of velocity. As all physics students know, velocity is speed in a certain direction. The Ball Screamer's speed was headed in the direction of Kayla Bateman's face.

I realized the car was about to fly into Kayla's face and cringed, and Ashley Milano realized and gasped, but neither Ashley nor I was faster than the Ball Screamer. It hurled the toy car into Kayla's face.

Instantly, Kayla raised her hand to her cheekbone, where the car had hit. Most of our physics class was laughing, and someone said, "Too bad it didn't hit her in the tits; she wouldn't've even felt it." I smiled rather than laughed, because in my pre-vampire life I probably would have been the one hit in the face. Still, it was pretty ridiculous to be injured by something called the Ball Screamer.

Then Kayla dropped her hand and we all saw that (a) she was crying and (b) she was bleeding. There was a deep gash under her eye and bright red blood was running down her face where tears should have been. Her hand had blood on it, too. I felt sick to my stomach, which probably made me very similar to the imaginary riders of the Ball Screamer.

"You're BLEEDING!" Ashley Milano shrieked.

"Oh, dear. Oh, dear. I'll get some gauze," said Einstein, rushing to her desk.

"I'm bleeding?" Kayla said anxiously. Then she raised her hand to her face and shrieked. "Oh, God, I'm bleeding!"

Then the class began to buzz with indistinct conversations, and THEN—everyone turned to look at me.

"What?" I asked. I actually asked it out loud. What was I supposed to do about Kayla's injury? I wasn't taking First Aid class. First Aid class was the only class wussier than Nutritional Science.

Then Kayla turned to look at me, too. And she let out the most incredible scream. Seriously, a horror-movie scream. It reverberated through the classroom and hallways. It was louder than any fire alarm I'd ever heard.

"What's going on here?" Einstein asked.

I wanted to know myself. I stared at Kayla, completely bewildered. But when I met her eyes, I saw this raw, primal fear. Where had I seen this look before?

Chris Perez. Chris Perez was scared of me like this. He was scared of me because I'm a vampire.

Kayla couldn't even speak. She pointed to me with a trembling hand, and Einstein, scurrying back with gauze in hand, asked, "What? What did Finbar do?"

For my part, I backed away nonthreateningly. I made every "safe" gesture I could think of. I held my hands up where Kayla could see them, like I was surrendering to the police. I crossed my hands in front of me, like I was an umpire above a runner sliding into home plate. I kept my distance from Kayla. But I was still looking at her. And I was still seeing all that blood gushing out of her face. Oh, God, that nonstop blood. *Don't think about how creepy it is. Don't think about how disgusting it is.*

But, only five feet from the door—my escape—I passed out.

As I became conscious slowly, I realized I was in the nurse's office. I could smell the scent of disinfectant and of girls faking migraines to skip gym. I also became aware of the doubtfulness that anyone believed I was a vampire anymore. Vampires didn't faint like Southern belles at the sight of blood. Shattering my own vampire myth could possibly be a good thing at this point. I meant to frighten guys like Chris Perez, but I didn't mean to frighten girls. I meant to *attract* girls.

"Finn?" Jenny whispered.

I opened my eyes and squinted. Jenny looked extra pale under the lights. And she looked legitimately worried, like I was a soap opera character in a coma.

"Hey," I said.

"Are you okay?" Jenny asked.

"Totally fine," I said. "Sorry about that."

"You kind of freaked everyone out," Jenny said.

"Did I?" I asked. "What happened?"

"No, no, no," Jenny reassured me. "Kayla got stitched up. And she's not scared of you anymore."

"What?" I tried to sit up. Some blood rushed to my head. Jesus. "How is she not scared of me anymore?"

"Ashley and I explained it to her," Jenny said. "You know, the reason you passed out."

"What?"

Once again, I was completely confused. Ashley and *Jenny*, Jenny, my biggest vampire groupie, had told Kayla that I was scared of blood and wasn't a vampire?

"Sure," Jenny explained. "We told her that you don't... you know, *eat your meals*...in school."

"What?"

"Well, isn't that why you don't have lunch with the rest of us?"

"Uh…"

"So," Jenny chirped brightly, "we told her you just passed out because you're hungry!"

I had to recover super fast from my fainting spell, because I had an important night that night after the roller coasters. I was going to dinner at Kate's house.

She'd claimed it was because her dad was a really good cook.

"He ordered all these new weird pots and he's cooking Thai food," Kate said. "Do you like Thai food?"

I was from Indiana. I'd never eaten Thai food.

"Yeah, I like it," I said.

"Good!" she said. "Come over tonight at, like, eight? You can meet my mom."

"Oh, okay, cool," I said, completely thrown. "Is…anyone else coming?"

"None of my siblings are home," Kate said. "So it will just be us and my parents."

"Oh," I said. "Cool."

"Is that okay?"

"Cool," I said again.

As I got dressed, I reminded myself that the more times you use the word *cool* in a five-minute conversation, the less cool you are. And I couldn't afford to be uncool tonight.

This was a very important night. This was a make-or-break night for me. Impressing Kate's parents could be a big step toward making me Kate's boyfriend. Actually, it was a make-or-break night for me because I didn't know if I was Kate's boyfriend. We'd gone out to a movie, and she'd acted like we were just friends. But I'd met her dad when I dropped her off. Then she'd kissed me in the hallway. The kiss wasn't even as important as where the kiss took place. This wasn't a back-porch, beer-smeared, hidden, drunken, mistake kind of kiss. It had been deliberate. It had been public. It had declared to people, "We are together!"

But were we together? As I drove to Kate's house, I stole glances in the rearview mirror, made serious faces, and asked my dashboard, "Where is this relationship going?" I practiced the words out loud: "Kate, would you be okay with calling me your boyfriend?" No, that seemed misogynistic and control-ling somehow. It should be, "Can I call you my girlfriend?"

No. All of that sounded lame. It sounded desperate. It sounded like I was trying too hard, which is exactly what I'd done wrong with Celine. As I pulled into the driveway, I resolved not to make the same mistake with Kate and her family.

It was Kate's dad who opened the door. We'd only met very briefly last time after the movie. Now I reasserted my impression with a super-firm and manly handshake.

"Mr. Gallatin," I said. "Thanks so much for having me."

"Nice to see you, Finbar," he said. "Here, come meet Janice."

I shook hands with Kate's mother—more gently. Both of Kate's parents were tall and thin. They were pretty old, too.

They had white hair and they weren't even trying to hide it, the way my mom hid her gray hair by dyeing it and my dad covered his bald spot with baseball caps that fooled no one. Kate's mom, Janice, wasn't a MILF, but that was preferable for me. MILFs kind of scare me. I don't know how to work garter belts and stockings. So a regular mom was preferable. Although, to give Kate's mom the benefit of the doubt, she probably was a MILF back when Kate's three older siblings were young. And if she had grandchildren soon, she could definitely be a GILF.

Oh, Jesus, what was I doing with all these lustful thoughts? Kate's parents were Catholic just like mine. Everyone knows Catholics have, like, X-ray vision for sexual thoughts. For example, freshman year at St. Luke's we had this amazingly hot English teacher, Ms. Alexander. She was a great teacher — in fact, I stopped thinking about her chest long enough to comprehend dangling modifiers — but she quit by November. This is because she had X-ray vision and could see all the perverted things we were all thinking about her.

Or maybe she got a hint from Johnny Frackas's "10 Goals for My Life" essay, which Sean O'Connor had stolen and written in a #11: "Do Ms. Alexander up the ass."

Anyway, I didn't want the Gallatins knowing all the thoughts I had about Kate. Not that I thought about #11. No way! What do you think of me? But I'm not gonna say I didn't think about Kate when I was in bed. Or in the shower. Or in the kitchen...

"You like it spicy, Finbar?" Kate's mother asked, poking her head out of the kitchen.

Huh? Spicy? I was startled in the living room where I was sitting on the couch next to Kate, clutching a glass of Pepsi. I began to sweat.

"Your Thai food?" Kate's mom asked. "Do you like it spicy?"

"Oh," I said, relieved. "Sure."

Kate raised her eyebrow at me. She could tell I was nervous.

Kate's parents popped in and out of the kitchen as they cooked. They were pretty easy to talk to. They asked me all about our move from Indiana. It turns out Mr. Gallatin had grown up in Illinois, and used to go white-water rafting not too far from Alexandria. Kate's parents had all these cool hobbies. They went camping and they had a kayak. They did things I'd only seen in Eddie Bauer catalogs. They asked if my parents had any hobbies. I don't think extreme cleaning is a sport yet, so I said my mom didn't.

"But my dad's thinking about taking up surfing," I said.

When Kate and I went into the dining room, I kind of regretted being so casual about the whole "do you like spicy food" thing, considering I usually ate food that was the same color as my skin. You know, popcorn, baked potatoes, unsauced chicken breasts. Now I was staring at a veritable after-school special of different colors and shapes climbing all over each other in joy. The steaming pot that Mr. Gallatin set on the table was a dish that he called Dragon Curry.

The Gallatins didn't say grace, so I couldn't put off this meal any longer. There were hunks of chicken on my plate covered in green and red flakes. The chicken smelled spicy, but maybe just those red and green flakes were spicy. When no one was looking, I scraped off the red flakes first. Then I began on the green, but Mr. Gallatin turned to speak to me and I panicked and popped the half-naked chicken into my mouth.

"So what makes a sophomore like Kate cool enough to hang out with you, Finbar?" Mr. Gallatin asked.

"She's—" I began. But the Dragon Curry flavor hit me.

I couldn't swallow. It was so, so freakin' hot. But I couldn't be rude, either, and spit the chicken out. When I opened my mouth again, the sting of my own breath made me gasp.

"Hot!" I exclaimed. "Oh, God, hot!"

Silence ensued. There had been the usual pleasant dinner noises of forks clinking on plates, ice in glasses, and of course the deadly hiss of the Dragon Curry in its lair. Now there was silence. Kate's father had asked me why I liked her and I had said, "She's...hot." Actually, I hadn't *said* the word *hot*, I'd *ejaculated* the word *hot*. I couldn't look at Kate's parents.

But I did glance briefly at Kate, turning my head with a tensed neck. Kate was laughing, silently, with her mouth full.

Mr. Gallatin spoke up.

"Well, Finbar," he said.

I looked up in dread, my face as red as the flakes I'd scraped from his chicken.

"You need some hot sauce on that?"

Kate's father and Kate both laughed at his joke, and I attempted to simultaneously laugh and sigh in relief, but Kate's mom rolled her eyes.

"You know when we were dating and I laughed at your jokes?" Mrs. Gallatin said to her husband. "I was faking it."

Now I laughed aloud. In that moment, Mrs. Gallatin was so unexpectedly bold and straightforward. She was so much like Kate.

"Maybe some rice will absorb the heat," Kate's dad said more practically. "I'll go get some."

When Kate's dad returned with rice, he said, "In all seriousness, Finbar, we're glad Kate has found a friend like you."

Well, I thought smugly. *More than a friend. Your daughter kissed me in the hallway. With a little bit of tongue.*

Of course, I didn't mention this.

Kate's father continued, "Someone who..."

Someone who is sexy? Dark and mysterious? No, he wouldn't say that. Someone who really cares for Kate? Someone who's become very close to our daughter? Was this leading into the boyfriend/girlfriend talk?

"Someone who's interested in schoolwork," Kate's father finished. "A really *nice kid.*"

My death knell had rung. Boom, boom, boom. Done, done, done. No more chance with Kate. That was the *worst* thing he could have possibly said! Wow, this dad was crafty. That comment was the verbal equivalent of a chastity belt. I wish he had said: "A kid with rampant acne." "A kid with incurable halitosis." "A kid looking at five to ten years in the state penitentiary."

Nothing could have ruined my chances faster with a high school girl than being labeled a *nice* kid. I thought this would be the night I found out whether or not I was Kate's boyfriend. Well, I guess I'd found out. A *nice kid* isn't a boyfriend. A *nice kid* is a friend.

Of course, I nodded and smiled. I hid my disappointment.

"Now for dessert," Kate's dad began. "We have another Thai specialty. An extra-spicy—"

Kate's mother interrupted, rolling her eyes. "We have ice cream. But Kate, why don't you show Finbar the Bat Cave while we clean up? You can eat dessert later."

Kate's "Bat Cave," which was their name for the basement, really rubbed the salt in the wound of our nonexistent romance. It was the coolest place in the world. My non-girlfriend was Batman. And I was her Alfred, pale and dependable. But seriously, back to this basement. They had a full-sized pool table, an air-hockey table, even a Skee-Ball machine. I was envious of Kate and her brother and sisters. And whoever would be Kate's boyfriend. I was pretty envious of him for a lot of reasons.

"We have the best movie channels," Kate told me when I went to sit next to her. Damn. What soft leather.

"I watch, like, six movies every weekend," she continued. "Oh my gosh, *Bloodthirsty* the movie is on. Have you ever seen it? This movie is hysterical. It's basically pornography."

On the screen, Virginia White, played by an anorexic model in a push-up bra, was spying on Chauncey Castle, some British "serious actor" with powder all over his face, as he examined vials of blood at his desk. After unscrewing the top of one of the vials, he brought it to his mouth and drank it. Virginia gasped and Chauncey turned around to catch her spying.

I turned to Kate and said, "I thought girls loved *Bloodthirsty*."

"They just like this movie because it's rated, like, triple X and they're not allowed to see it." Kate rolled her eyes. "It's *forbidden*."

I tried to look dark and dangerous. "Do you like forbidden things?" I asked.

"No," Kate said flatly.

"Well, what about *Bloodthirsty* the book?" I asked. "Girls definitely love the book."

"The girls in *your* class love it," Kate told me. "People didn't even know Ashley Milano could read until *Bloodthirsty* came out. And Kayla Bateman fell off the elliptical machine because she was reading the handcuff scene."

"Maybe she was just top-heavy," I suggested.

"Oh my God, that reminds me!" Kate said, sitting up cross-legged on the leather. "I wanted to tell you something *hysterical* that I heard Jenny Beckman saying."

Oh, God, what was it? Jenny was around me way too much. She could have said anything about me. No, calm down. Maybe it wasn't about me. Where was this unnatural belief that I was the center of the universe coming from?

"She and Kayla Bateman were talking about you, and…"

Uh-oh. Uh-oh. It was about me. Had I been caught in a Nate Kirkland moment? But I only ever scratched my nose in public! Never picked! It had been a scratch, I swear!

"They, like, think you're a vampire," Kate said. She waited, smiling, expectant, as if she'd just finished the punch line of a joke.

My first thought was, *Duh, of course I'm a vampire.* The

knowledge was pretty widespread now. Ashley Milano had even lent me the sun shield from her Oldsmobile to protect my skin when I walked to the parking lot. And the girls who had started with garlic bread had since approached me with a silver crucifix and a stick that vaguely resembled a wooden stake. While I was glad these girls believed I was a vampire, I was also kinda bummed out they were trying to kill me.

"Oh." I pushed a pathetic laugh up from my stomach.

Kate, expecting me to give a full-belly laugh of the type perfected by Santa Claus, recognized the lameness of my reaction. Damn my weakness for smart girls.

"You knew they thought that?" she asked.

"I don't know, I mean, I heard something," I said. "But uh, obviously, I thought it was a joke."

"Didn't you think it was *completely ridiculous*?" Kate said, opening her eyes wide at me.

"Yeah, I guess...." I shrugged and looked back toward the screen.

Chauncey Castle was drizzling blood down Virginia's chest and then licking it off. In between moans, Virginia told him: *I know that you are dangerous. But my passion for you is dangerous, too.*

"So why didn't you tell them you're...a human?" Kate asked. She was grinning broadly and, as she thought of me as a vampire, she burst out laughing. She even threw her head back.

"Oh." I shrugged again. My shoulders were getting sore from all this shrugging. "I mean, there were a lot of people who thought...or assumed...like..."

185

"Really?" Kate said. "I thought maybe Jenny just told Kayla, because Jenny's a little, ya know…"

"So," I ventured weakly to Kate. "You didn't think I was… a vampire?"

Kate laughed louder than an entire audience at *The Colbert Report*. Her laughter was enormous, taking up all the space in the room, and I was suddenly very, very small.

"Are you kidding?" she asked. "Did you *want* me to—"

"But," I ventured, "what about my sun thing?"

"What?"

"You didn't think it was weird that I can't go out in the sun?" I nudged.

"Aren't you Irish?"

"But you didn't think I was…dark and mysterious?"

"You drive a Volvo."

"Edward Cullen drives a Volvo!" I jumped up in my own defense.

"Did you buy that car to be like Edward Cullen?" Kate asked.

"No!" I said. "My dad liked the gas mileage…but, wait. You didn't think I was a vampire? Or that I was, like, scary? Or that I beat people up all the time?"

Kate shook her head. "Not even close," she told me with a certainty that made me depressed.

"So…but…"

I tried to think for a minute, but on the screen Virginia White's blood was being sucked out. Her semi-horrified, semi-orgasmic moans distracted me.

"But what?" Kate prompted.

"So why did you, like, you know…in the hallway…?"

"What?"

"Why did you kiss me?" I asked. "Why do you…did you… whatever…*like* me, if you don't think I'm scary or a vampire or beat people up all the time?"

"I like you because you're *not* scary," she said, still smiling. Kate raised the remote to switch off the TV, then turned to face me. "Or a vampire. And because you don't beat people up all the time. And because you're not an asshole like Chris Perez."

She put down the remote. She moved closer to me on the leather couch. She swung one knee around to the other side of my legs. She straddled me. Oh, wow. Oh, wow. She kissed me.

"Hold on one second," I said, now speaking with difficulty considering the new direction in which the blood in my body was rushing. "Now that you no longer think I'm mysterious, will you do me a favor?"

"What is it?"

But then she tugged at her lip with her teeth, and I saw her parted teeth, soft tongue, all that pink wetness.

"It can wait till later," I said, grinning, and leaned in.

The next time I saw Kate at school, after a hug at my locker that brought back memories of making out in the Bat Cave for an hour and a half, I asked Kate to tutor Luke. And I promised her that my mom would pay her—or, probably, *canonize* her, as long as she could keep Luke in the Fordham Prep varsity sports program. Of course, Kate offered to do it for free.

"I'm really interested to meet your brother!" Kate told me.

Super. Fantastic. I couldn't wait for her to meet my hunky heartthrob brother either. Seriously.

I told my mother that I'd found Luke a tutor.

"Who?" my mother asked. "That boy Jason you've told me about?"

"No," I said. "My friend Kate."

"Kate whose house you went to for dinner Kate?" my mother asked, leaning in to me like she was a witch and I was Hansel covered in candy.

"Yeah," I said. "She's pretty good at math."

In my mind, I was the essence of smooth during this conversation (although I shouldn't waste my smoothness on my mother. But I guess vampires have so much of it that I can use a little bit of smoothness on my mother). But my mom had a goofy grin on her face, and I knew she thought Kate and I were in love. My mother has a sixth sense about these things.

And so Kate came to my house two nights later. And she met my whole family: my brother, who once used our Waterford crystal dessert plates as Frisbees; my mother, five foot nothing, armed with a Swiffer mop and waaaay too in the loop about my feelings for Kate; and my father, who was still eagerly asking me for details of what it was like to be in a fight.

My dad was the first one to meet her.

"Kate!" he boomed in that cheesy sitcom-dad voice. "Nice to meet you, Kate!"

Why is it that parents repeat someone's name eight times

when they meet them? It must be their fading memories. My parents are middle-aged, after all. They're not as sharp as they once were.

"Well, is this Finbar's Kate or Luke's Kate?"

Asking that was my dad's next stupid move. Way to objectify women, Dad!

But Kate shrugged, seemingly unoffended.

"I'm usually Finbar's," she said. "But today I'm Luke's. For geometry proofs. Lucky him."

"You know," my dad said thoughtfully, "I never had to prove a damned thing when I was in school! They told me two plus two was four, I just believed what they told me."

"Paul! Did I just hear bad language in here? From *you*?"

My mother came scurrying out of the kitchen with an enormous bottle of Lysol All Purpose Cleaner. She aimed the spray nozzle at my dad like it was a gun. I swear, she would have cleaned his mouth with it if I hadn't interrupted.

"Mom!" I called, my tense tone hopefully indicating she should behave herself. "This is Kate. She's gonna help Luke with his math homework."

"Oh, Kate!" my mother squealed.

My mother got overly excited and prematurely ejaculated some Lysol into Kate's face. Right there in the front hall, I put my face in my hands and groaned.

My mother rushed to Kate's side.

"Thank God for your glasses!" she was squeaking. "I could have blinded you!"

"I told you, the house is clean enough!" my father said.

My mother was furiously wiping Kate's glasses on her own shirt. Then my mother put her glasses on for her. Like Kate couldn't do it herself!

"What beautiful hair you have," my mother cooed, like the Big Bad Wolf talking to Red Riding Hood. I was surprised Kate hadn't bolted from my house by now.

"Mom—" I tried to form a buffer between her and Kate.

"I always thought I'd have a daughter," my mother began to reflect. "When I found out I was having twins, they told me it was a boy and a girl."

Oh, God no. Please let a terrorist come along and *gag* my mother right now.

"From the sonogram, they could tell Luke was a boy," my mother explained. "But from the way Finbar was positioned, you couldn't even tell he had a—"

"Luke!" I exclaimed.

I'd never been so ecstatic to introduce my good-looking, athletic brother to a girl I liked.

Luke pounded down the stairs as usual and jumped the last three. He extended his hand.

"You're Kate, right?" Luke flashed his non-creepy blue eyes at the girl I liked. "Thanks for coming over."

My mom steered them to the dining room, and I went upstairs to my room because I didn't want to hang around. But I was so anxious about how Kate and Luke were getting along that I even crouched down and pressed my ear to the floor. Too bad my mother's vacuum was sucking out all possibility of eavesdropping. Acting like Luke, I jumped around the room and then lay in his bed and threw his Nerf balls at the ceiling. I hit a spiderweb and it fell on my face. Gross.

I tried to tell myself I had nothing to worry about. I mean, really. Sure, Luke's good-looking. Sure, Luke's in pretty good shape. He could probably bench-press an elephant if he had to. But to be honest, my brother doesn't have a whole lot of game. He has the pickup skills of a hurricane. Sure, he's big and exciting and energetic, and sure, everyone talks about him on the local news, and maybe some girls get all caught up in him and follow him wherever he's going, but Luke is a wild and unpredictable force. Not even he has control over his own power. If he set out with the intention to seduce a particular girl, he wouldn't have the skill for it. He wouldn't have the attention for it. He wouldn't succeed.

Would he?

Under the very sneaky pretense of having an apple, I went downstairs. An apple would give me an excuse to spy on Kate and Luke *and* would prove to Kate that I was healthy. In biology, we learned that a lot of "attractive" traits are actually biologically alluring because they mean we're healthy as potential mates. I'd just stroll in, apple in hand, wordlessly bragging about my mating ability, my strong teeth and fast-moving bowels...

But they were laughing. From the staircase landing in the front hall, I could hear them laughing. Shit. Laughing? What was funny about Math B, I wondered as I walked back to the dining room. I'd never taken Math B, but it was math, and math was never fun. Even that show *Numb3rs*, which tries to make math cool, is on every Friday night, because people who like math are always home on Friday nights!

Oh, no. I bet it was Luke. Luke had made Kate laugh.

"Done!" Kate cried from the dining room.

"Done! No, you beat me!" Luke cried right after her. He laughed.

I entered with the caution of a crime scene investigator. Luke and Kate were sitting side by side, but their chairs were turned more toward each other than toward the table, where the books, notebooks, and things they *should* have been focusing on were.

"Hey, guys," I said. "So...what's going on here?"

Luke snatched Kate's paper and looked rapidly from hers back to his.

"Dammit!" He slapped his head, then slumped in his seat, pretending to drop dead. "I forgot to say that this thing equals that thing. But I know it does. So why do I have to say it?"

"You just do," Kate said. "All the obvious stuff. Otherwise you can't get from step one to step two. Which means, I am the champion!"

She threw both hands in the air.

"Champion of what?" I asked.

"We're racing through proofs," Luke told me. "Kate beat me three times in a row."

"And loser has to copy the proof over," Kate said. "Three times."

Luke groaned, and Kate passed him an empty notebook and a pen. "There ya go, sucker," she said.

While Luke copied the proof in his manic handwriting, Kate looked up, winked at me, and smiled. I smiled back genuinely and leaned against the doorway. It seemed somehow natural, Kate here in my dining room, at the table where we ate corned beef every Tuesday, below the childhood pictures in which Luke and I were wearing matching reindeer sweaters. In the second picture, he stuck his finger in my ear and in the third picture I had my face so scrunched up you couldn't see my eyes. But I wasn't embarrassed for her to see me as a puny, tackily dressed child. I couldn't lose my sense of mystery because, according to Kate, I never had one.

Wasn't it ironic? I'd made myself a vampire so I could get girls to like me. Now the one girl I cared about didn't even like vampires. And she didn't like me because I was moody, mysterious, or scary. She liked me because I wasn't like that at all.

"Ready?" Luke said to Kate, ready to rip right through the pages.

She said, "Ready, set, go."

chapter

All my high school life, I've had this hypothesis that you can't go to a party unless you have a reason to be there. I've never actually been to a real party. I've only been to those sweet sixteens where the guy's mom makes him invite everyone in the class, even the kids who don't speak English. But I think at *real* parties, house parties, you have to have a reason to be there. For example, Luke is on the football team. This means that he gets invited to a lot of victory celebrations, especially because he usually is the reason for the victory. Also, he's very strong. So he's useful in lifting kegs and breaking open back windows to flee the cops and such. Also, when Luke goes to a party, girls go to a party.

Other guys have different reasons. Often the biggest schmuck in your class will have the greatest house and the most wonderful absentee parents, so he'll get to throw the parties. That's a hell of a reason to be at a party — when it's in your own house. Then there's the kid who's got the older brother or creepy uncle who buys the beer; he's the supplier. Then there's the kid with all the stolen hip-hop music on his iPod; he's the DJ. If there's a kid who's kind of on the border, a kid who's a backup on the basketball team, a kid who's a little overweight, a kid who wears boat shoes without socks, there's one quality that can endear him to other guys and hot girls alike: "But he's, like, *so* funny."

And girls? No. Girls don't need a reason to be at a party. Girls *are* the reason to be at a party.

The week after Halloween, Luke invited Kate and me to a football party in New Rochelle, which was halfway between Pelham and Kate's town of Larchmont. Every other time that Luke had invited me to a party, I had refused to go. But now everything was different. Now, beyond having my brother as the kickass running back, I had a reason to go. I was bringing a girl.

The party house was huge, right on the water, with a big front porch and big backyard. It was Luke's teammate's house. Luke had been there before and showed us around. The party was already in progress when we arrived, i.e., most people were already drunk. There were girls trying to dance in the living room even though they couldn't hear the music over their own laugher. The tallest one tried to break-dance to a John Mayer song. When her handstand failed, she spilled Smirnoff Ice down her push-up bra. Then she began to cry, and the other girls surrounded her in a kind of emotional huddle.

The iPod DJ was pretty nerdy; he had these thick, black-rimmed glasses that weren't even hip in the Rivers Cuomo way. *Score*, I thought, *I'm cooler than someone at this party*. But, although he looked wimpy, he put up a pretty good fight when a girl lectured him with a pointing finger and a sloshing cup. "You should *not* play any Chris Brown songs," the girl told the DJ. "I'm serious. Like, as a woman."

"I'm sorry." The DJ shook his head. "'Forever' is just too good to pass up."

"'Forever' was the single that was out when the whole thing happened!" The girl was outraged. "That's, like, the *worst* one to pick."

"Yeah, but I made up a dance to it," the DJ said. He stood up and popped and locked and dropped a little bit. He was actually a pretty good dancer. I was still cooler than him, though.

On the back porch, guys in black puffy North Face jackets were smoking cigarettes and acting shady. In the garage, the juniors and seniors were playing beer pong. I'd heard some senior guys at St. Luke's talk about beer pong, and I'm pretty sure Luke had played once or twice, but I didn't understand the game. How could you drink beer while playing ping-pong? That's how I thought you played, holding a bottle of beer in your left hand and your ping-pong paddle in your right hand.

But the beer was in red plastic cups, not bottles, and the cups were grouped together in triangle shapes on the surface of the ping-pong table. There were no paddles, but there were ping-pong balls—the guys just used their hands to throw the balls into the cups of beer. There were only guys playing. It looked like this was a "no girls allowed" zone. Backed two cautious feet from the testosterone-laden and splintered wood table, the girls stood in twos or threes, in jean skirts, gnawing at the rims of their own red plastic cups. Somehow, even though they didn't play, the girls knew a lot about the rules of the game. But how many rules could there be for throwing a ball in a cup?

"His elbow was a millimeter over the edge of the table! That shot doesn't count."

"His partner didn't say he was 'heating up' after the second shot sunk but before the opponent's turn began. He won't get the ball back upon sinking a third consecutive shot."

Apparently, there were more rules than I thought!

"Do you know how to play beer pong?" I asked Kate as we stood on the sidelines watching, holding red plastic cups. Ours contained Mountain Dew, though; Luke had poured our nonalcoholic drinks in the kitchen while he got himself a beer.

Kate shook her head.

I quickly resolved to go home that very night and learn beer pong. Once I was a master, I could beat seniors, and Kate would be impressed. So how would I get good? Luke would practice shots with me. I'd find a piece of wood for a table and we could sacrifice Luke's desk, which he never used anyway, to practice. We'd fill cups with water. I figured we'd get about two weeks of practice in before my mother discovered the cups in triangular formation and assumed we had joined a satanic cult. Yes, we were rehearsing for a game that involved drinking beer, and we were underage, but I knew my mom's mind would leap first to satanic cult.

Of course, I had never even had a beer. Maybe you had to learn how to drink beer before you learned how to play.

Or maybe if you drank too much beer, you couldn't play at all: none of these guys were actually getting their ping-pong balls in the cups of beer. So it was a pretty boring game to watch. The only entertaining thing was watching girls try to chase and retrieve the stray balls from the cobwebbed corners of the garage without bending over too far in their short skirts.

"Is this cup of water really used to clean the ball?" Kate asked, peering over the edge of the table at a red cup of water with a dirty clump of hair floating on its surface. "I don't think it's working."

"We probably got swine flu just by watching this game," I said. "Should we go see if the iPod DJ is still playing Chris Brown?"

"I think we should go to the kitchen and see your brother do a kegstand," she said. "He'll make it into an Olympic sport."

Kate led the way up the basement steps, and I had my hand on her back, possessive yet cool about it, when — *Bang!* The door swung open in front of us and hit a beam of the garage wall. This wasted kid who couldn't even see in front of him stumbled into the garage. Kate and I both backed up, because he stumbled down all three basement steps. Then he stopped, turned to us, and rocked back and forth, back on his heels, forward on his toes. Back on his heels, forward...

Rocking Chair pointed to Kate, his finger reaching forward out of his drunken stupor.

"Hey," he said. His eyelids drooped down over his eyes. "I know you," he told Kate.

Kate stood still, like she was hoping not to be noticed. Thinking this kid didn't even know who he was pointing to (or where he was), I led the way up the stairs again, took the first step, but—

"Katie," Rocking Chair said loudly, over the sound of a runaway beer pong ball and the girls shrieking over it. "Katie Gallatin."

"Kate?" I began. How did this creepy guy know Kate? This chest-filling, defensive, masculine thing took hold of me. Possession. As Bill Compton from *True Blood* always snarled in his fiercest Southern drawl, Kate was *mine*. Why was this loser even speaking to *my* Kate?

Tilting back, Rocking Chair snickered and said, "I don't recognize you with your clothes on."

I'd never seen Kate unsure before. Now she seemed flustered, even nervous. Her hand rose to adjust her hair, her glasses, and she looked down at the basement floor.

Rocking Chair only got louder. He called out, "Hey, I went to school with this girl in Larchmont." He pointed to Kate. "This girl was the biggest slut. Katie Gallatin was the biggest—"

"Hey!" I stepped in front of the shrunken, uncertain Kate. I almost tripped on the first basement step, but didn't. I was a big strong man. I was protecting the girl I loved—or, the girl I liked a hell of a lot. I was freakin' Edward Cullen staring down a werewolf.

Rocking Chair simply stepped to the side and kept speaking to Kate.

"Go get another drink, Katie," he told her. "Pass out and get the cops called to *this* party."

"Hey!" I said louder. Maybe my first "hey" hadn't been loud enough.

The nervous, buzzy feeling through my body wasn't quite the same powerful rush I had felt with Chris Perez. There, I'd been alone, no one except Chris Cho to see me make a fool of myself. Here I was surrounded by cool juniors and seniors from another school.

But I had to defend Kate. I didn't have to kick this guy's ass, just keep him separated from my girlfriend. I mean, the girl who is my friend. And who kissed me in the hallway, but may or may not have been romantically interested in me. But probably was.

So when Rocking Chair rocked a little too far forward, I extended a hand between us. He barely registered my movement. In fact, the kid was pretty out of it. He was looking like one of those after-school specials where your brain turns into scrambled eggs because you accepted a joint from a sketchy tempter at a chain-link fence. His eyelids were slipping lower, lower. He was about to pass out—

He punched me in the nose. Caught totally off guard, I was knocked off the first step. I fell to my hands and knees on the basement floor.

"Fuck you, Swanstein!" someone in the basement cried out. "You sucker punched that kid!"

"You're a douche bag, Swanstein!" someone else said. I heard the beer pong ball bounce away, abandoned, heard some heels shuffle over in the sawdust. I heard two different girls ask if I was all right; neither was Kate.

I could hear things going on, but I couldn't see. Everything went black and numb for those two seconds after the punch. Then the full impact of pain thrust through my face like the blade of a sword, from my nose deep into my skull. The sword of pain stayed plunged in my face; it took up residence there and throbbed. *Jesus. Christ.* In my head, those words repeated in time to the throbbing. *Jee. Zus. Christ.* Fuck that stoner! When I was able to get up from my knees, I swore, I would Chris Perez him and more. I would go straight for the blood supply and I wouldn't let go. I would...

My fury forced my eyes open. This was a moment where I expected to turn into the Hulk. Seriously, rip the seams of my polo shirt and let that little...

Oh, God. Oh my God. Blood. When I raised my chest and looked down, it was spilled over my shirt, arms, and hands, like someone had thrown a bucket of paint at me. There were black fisted clots in it, there were dark swirls pooling at the insides of my bent elbows as I raised my hands from the ground and drew them in toward my body. God. God. And I felt wet and cool at my nose—which meant the blood was still flowing. I raised my hands to my face and the blood flowed through my fingers. It was a volcano, erupting again and again, unforgiving.

I gave my intestines a mental pep talk: stay cool, guys. Keep it tight. No need to puke here in front of everyone, really, it's all right. I closed my eyes until I felt I could stand, trying to ignore how wet and sticky and covered I was.

When I stood up, Kate was gone.

I looked around, confused, scanning the whispering girls and the senior boys shaking their heads, but not registering any of their faces. I barely noticed that someone had gotten Luke; I heard him pounding down the sawdusted stairs. He was heading not for me, but for Rocking Chair kid, who was inexplicably bent over by the closest part of the beer pong table. What was wrong with him? No one had punched *him*!

"What the fuck, Swanstein?" Luke demanded. "I'm *talking* to you."

Luke gave him this cold stare and Swanstein looked up from the ground. And, get this—Swanstein was *crying*.

Luke was merciless, though.

"You fucking lay a hand on my brother again," Luke threatened. "Or you pussy punch any kid anywhere, and I'll really give you something to cry about. Did you hear me?"

Swanstein seriously had tears coming down his face! I watched in amazement. Seeing girls cry makes me very uncomfortable, but a fellow male in tears, in public, was pure fascination. I wanted to get a front-row seat and put on some 3-D glasses for the show.

"Did you hear me?" Luke barked louder. The party went still and silent. Luke enunciated every word. He said, "I. Would. Kill. You."

One of Luke's lazier friends told Swanstein, "You weren't even invited, man. We just called you for weed."

The word *weed* perked up one of the senior guys, who remembered why my Rocking Chair aggressor was there in the first place.

A merciful jean-skirt-clad girl came down the steps next to me, holding two paper towels. She handed them to me, but then backed away, clearly grossed out.

But Luke came over and stepped right on the bloody sawdust in front of the first step. He tilted my head up, his knuckles under my chin.

"You all right?" he asked.

I felt dizzy. "Yeah. Lots of blood, though…"

"The head always bleeds a lot," Luke told me. "Remember when I fell from the chandelier?"

I smiled through my nausea. "Yeah."

"And from that third-story window?"

"Yeah."

"And from the flagpole of our Montessori school?"

"I remember." I managed a small laugh. "But I'm surprised you do."

"Frame!" one of the seniors called from the beer pong table.

We both looked up.

The senior laughed. "I forgot there were two Frames. Luke Frame, that is. Next game?"

"I'm gonna play with Finn," Luke said.

"Nah," I interrupted. "I'm going to find Kate."

"'Kay," Luke said. "But when you come back, find me. We'll switch shirts."

"What?" I asked. "I'm covered in blood."

"Yeah," Luke said. "But Mom will be less freaked out if it's me. I've come home covered in blood before."

Kate wasn't in the living room, or the kitchen, or anywhere near the bathroom, where some girl was throwing up and another girl was choreographing it. "Here, you tie her hair back. You get a glass of water. You get a garbage bag." Kate wasn't in the backyard either when I stepped past the suspicious North Face congress. I walked down the driveway to get to the front yard, and there she was, at the end of the driveway, standing beneath a street lamp with her arms crossed.

She looked cold — she hadn't brought her jacket. I looked down. I looked like I'd wandered off the set of a Tarantino movie. No jacket to give her.

"Kate!" I called.

She turned briefly. In the light of the street lamp she had reached, her eyes looked big and wet. She wasn't crying yet, but she was close. Oh, God.

I jogged across the damp lawn to her.

"Are you okay?" she asked numbly, in a strange monotone.

"I'm fine," I said. "What happened? Who was that guy?"

"Swanstein," Kate said, wiping her nose on her sleeve. "We went to Larchmont together. But I left because…"

I stood, waiting patiently, cold, wet, bloody.

"I got in trouble," Kate said, looking me straight in the eyes. "I drank too much at a party and I had to get my stomach pumped. The cops came to the party and everyone got in trouble. Everyone at school hated me for it."

Even the last part she said coldly, steadily, rapidly, and without emotion.

"I'm not who you think I am," Kate continued, confessing at a faster and faster rate. "At Larchmont, I was a party girl. I wanted everyone to know who I was, so I started drinking more than all the other freshman girls. And doing more stuff with guys…"

Doing more stuff with guys. What stuff? I felt sickened at the thought of pickle flips and other foreign acts.

"Wait." I realized something terrible. "That picture in your locker. That wasn't your sister."

Kate bit her lip.

"That was you."

A guy came out of the house and performed an interpretive dance of how I was feeling right now. He stumbled down the steps, fell down, and puked all over himself.

"You lied to me," I said to Kate, planting my feet in the gravel between the paved driveway and the street.

She looked at me desperately, hands at her sides, unable to speak.

"You said you came to our school to take AP classes," I continued, louder. "You said you didn't drink."

"Finn…"

"I thought you didn't care about parties and beer and all that b.s. high school stuff," I said.

"I'm sorry, Finbar," Kate said. "But, I mean, to be fair, you kind of lied to me, too."

"What?" I went from disbelieving to angry very quickly.

Kate crossed her arms over her chest, and I couldn't tell if it was a defensive move or from the cold.

"Well, you're not a *vampire*," she told me.

"Jesus, Kate." I rolled my eyes and stomped at the curb. "That is so ridiculous. That is so completely different."

"Why?" Kate challenged me, stepping closer.

"I never told anyone I was a vampire," I said, looking down at her. My position on the curve of the pavement gave me extra height above her as she stood in the street.

"But people *believed* you were."

"And I believed you!" I yelled back, so suddenly and forcefully that Kate rocked back on her heels.

That was *exactly* the point. I'd believed Kate. Of course, on the outside, she was beautiful and confident, which I saw at first glance. But then we got to know each other. And she told me that she loved math. That she didn't know that many people at school. That she liked to read. That she stayed home on

Friday nights to watch movies. And I thought, as beautiful as she was on the outside, on the inside she was kind of sensitive. Maybe a loner. Maybe like...

"I believed you were like me," I spit out. "You made me believe that."

I don't know how she reacted. I looked down at my sneakers instead, and I couldn't look back up. I was pissed off and I pushed gravel from the ground into the toe of my shoe, tearing the rubber.

Still, in a final, painful, lame nice-guy gesture, I asked Kate, "Do you need me to walk you to the train?"

I asked it detachedly, my arms crossed. Dumb move. I smeared extra blood all over myself.

Kate shook her head. "My sister's coming. She's going to pick me up."

I trudged back to the house. Still wet with blood, I looked as if she'd really ripped my heart out of my chest—and then thrown it back at me and stained my shirt. The worst part was that this was how it was supposed to be. I mean, Kate belonged out on Friday nights, at parties, doing pickle flips and kegstands. She belonged with other guys. I, meanwhile, belonged on the couch next to my mom, waiting for the Bennet sisters to get married off. Parties, beer, rule-breaking, romance—these weren't things for me. The worst part was knowing the whole thing had been a joke.

Actually, the worst part was that I stepped in that kid's vomit on the way back inside.

Back inside to say good-bye to my brother, to leave forever his world, to return home to the safe boundaries of my mom-sanitized walls, my whiny amateur poems, my fantasies.

"Hey, Finbar!" Luke's shadow on the front steps was holding a beer. "Time for our game!"

Okay, I guess my sailor bedsheets and the Bennet sisters could wait. I had to wait for Luke's bloodless shirt anyway. And so I played beer pong. And drank real beer. And, actually, I did well. Beginner's luck, I guess. I sank quite a few cups, and we beat two different teams.

I guess a guy with vomit on his feet, blood on his shirt, and tears in his eyes is pretty intimidating to an opponent.

chapter

I thought the world would end when Kate and I broke up. But I'd also thought the world would end when Kate told me she knew I wasn't a vampire, or when I passed out in physics class, and it hadn't. You may not have noticed this, but I can be a pessimist sometimes. But I shouldn't be. I mean, I've had the name *Finbar* for sixteen years, and I've only been punched in the face once.

After my surprisingly kick-ass game of beer pong that night (Luke and I killed. We should have been playing for money!), I steeled myself to return home and break the news to my mother that Kate and I were no longer...whatever Kate and I had been. But I was actually able to avoid lengthy conversations with my mother for that whole week and so didn't have that much time to sit around like a hunchback ringing the death knell of my love life. After school, I'd begun training for winter track. Jason Burke was my training buddy. I was pleased to find he wasn't in as great shape as I'd assumed. I think his muscles were just more defined because he had a spray tan.

In my spare time when I wasn't running, I was catching up with Jenny. I felt bad. I'd kind of forgotten about her during the whole Kate thing. And I didn't even remember that I had forgotten her until she invited me to a book signing but followed the invitation with, "But you're probably busy on a Saturday night. Doing something with Kate."

"I'm not," I said. "Kate and I aren't really hanging out anymore."

"Really?" Jenny squeaked in delight.

Jeez, she really wanted to go to this book signing. She sounded ecstatic. Of course, she was mildly obsessed with this book. When we met up late Saturday afternoon and took a train into the city, Jenny chattered the whole time about the author and the book. The book was a "graphic novel," which is a term that adults have created so they can read comic books when they're middle-aged. Except this graphic novel didn't have any superheroes, sidekicks, or anything that should have been on a five-year-old boy's underwear. The author was this Irish guy who drew amazing pictures of his life in Dublin, drinking Guinness, chain-smoking, cheering for his hometown soccer team, and other manly Irish things.

I think of Irish guys as real men's men, always drinking really heavy beer without throwing up and then punching some English guy's crooked teeth out because they're frustrated with centuries of colonialism. And playing rugby. Rugby doesn't have shoulder pads *or* helmets. My ancestors were Irish, but somehow we got more wussed out with each passing generation. Although Luke would probably kick ass at rugby.

Jenny, who from the looks of her wouldn't survive five seconds of rugby, got a special invite to the book signing because she wrote a review of the book for our school newspaper. Usually Jenny's reviews don't get published because she refuses to write about any movie with Vince Vaughn or Seth Rogen in it or to profile any Disney Channel starlet caught topless via text message. But the editor liked this graphic novel review because it had so much beer in it. I think our school newspaper editor has a drinking problem. It must be the stress of his job.

Anyway, Jenny had sent the author, Gareth, a copy of her review, which he loved, so we got to meet him before the event started at a bookstore in midtown Manhattan.

"Jenny!" Gareth crowed when she introduced herself shyly. "I've got to thank you for that piece you wrote on me. It's the only nice thing that's been written about me, other than stuff on the pub bathroom wall."

Jenny flushed.

"Seriously, brilliant stuff, though," he said.

Jenny introduced me, and Gareth was surprised by my name.

"I don't meet many American Finbars," he told me.

"I'm pretty sure I'm the only one," I said.

"The Celt stands alone," Gareth said. "Well, I should get reading. Get good seats, but not in the front row. Ya don't want me spitting on you."

Jenny seemed nervous around Gareth and she hurried me away. She pulled me so fast that I didn't have time to look where I was going, and I bumped into a different short girl.

"Finbar!" the short girl exclaimed.

"Oh," I said. "Hi, Celine."

Surprisingly, I hadn't thought about Celine in a while. After our disastrous date, I had expected to stew over the humiliation for months. But I'd been so busy being a vampire and starting at a new school and getting rejected by a whole new girl that I'd forgotten about Celine.

She looked the same, small and brown and sharp-looking. I couldn't remember why I'd thought she was so pretty. Compared to Kate, Celine looked like she'd sucked a sour lemon. She pressed that sour-lemon face to mine and gave me a lame French air kiss.

"How are you, *chérie?*" she twittered. "I haven't heard from you in ages!"

"I know," I said. "I've been...this is Jenny. Jenny, Celine."

"*Enchanté,*" Celine said affectedly.

"You, too...I think," Jenny replied.

"We should go grab seats," I told Celine. "Nice to see you."

"Who was that?" Jenny hissed before we were even out of earshot.

"Just a girl I went out with once," I said.

Wow. I couldn't believe that phrase just came out of my mouth. "A girl I went out with once." That made it sound like I went out with lots of girls. I sounded so...McDreamy. Or McSteamy. Yeah, more like McSteamy, because he got more action (yes, sadly, I do know the difference between McDreamy and McSteamy. Again, my mother's fault).

"Did you like her?" Jenny asked.

Jenny would make a great reporter. She always asks a lot of questions. This particular question made me think, though. And when I thought about it, Celine had been elitist and obnoxious and ungrateful. She used these French phrases, probably to make me feel dumb—obviously she was still doing it. Furthermore, Celine had never thanked me for the ridiculously expensive meal I had bought her. Whether or not I had tried too hard, I deserved at least a thank you.

"Not really," I told Jenny as we took our seats. "I mean, I didn't like her as much as I liked Kate."

Jenny swallowed. "Oh," was all she said, then she shut up like a clam.

Luckily I didn't have to talk to Celine again, because Gareth started reading and telling stories. He was really funny. All the girls in the audience were going crazy because of his Irish accent. *Maybe I should pretend to be foreign,* I thought suddenly. *I bet I could get a lot of girls that way.* Then I remembered I was still kind of busy pretending to be the last thing I had pretended to be to get girls—a vampire.

For some reason, as Jenny and I walked back to Grand Central Station to take the train home, the city seemed quieter than usual. Actually, it wasn't quiet at all—it was midtown Manhattan on a Saturday night. But it seemed quiet to me, even as I watched the characters around us. Two self-centered women fought over a cab.

"I can't walk! I have six Bloomingdale's bags!" the first woman screamed.

"*I* can't walk! Look at my shoes!" said the second, displaying a heel too dangerous to make it through airport security.

Two guys who looked younger than I did came tumbling out of a darkened bar called the Lace Lounge. A bouncer the size of Canada told them, "Don't come back!" before slamming the door. The two guys proceeded to fight about what had given them away as underage.

"It's because you can't grow a mustache!" the first guy said.

"No," the other argued. "It's because *you* brought your little brother."

"Hey, guys! Wait up!" a smaller voice called. When the two guys parted, I could see a ten-year-old trailing along behind them.

I grinned as we walked past the underage kids and came upon a tall street performer guy singing early Mariah Carey hits in a surprisingly convincing voice. Wow, he was really hitting those high notes! Wow, he...might be a she. Or was it a he? Or was it...

I was about to ask for Jenny's input when I realized what was making it seem quiet. *Jenny* was quiet. And that was such a rare occurrence that it threw me off completely. Refraining from asking for her input on the diva's gender ambiguity, I put my hands in my pockets, and Jenny trudged along next to me. Usually she'd be tugging at my sleeves, asking me a million questions, talking about the reading. But she wasn't saying anything.

When I looked to the side and opened my mouth to make conversation, I saw the reflection of a streetlight streaming down Jenny's face. She was crying! What the hell? Why was Jenny crying? More important, what was I supposed to do about it? I turned my head away quickly. Maybe she didn't want to be seen crying. I wouldn't want anyone to see me crying. I would want everyone around me to ignore the situation completely.

Jenny didn't want that. When I turned my head away from her, she sniffed pointedly.

Maybe I just had to change the subject, and she would forget whatever had made her cry. It couldn't have been that big a deal anyway if I hadn't noticed Jenny get upset (and I *had* noticed that transvestite singing Mariah Carey songs).

"That Gareth guy was pretty funny," I said. "You know, when he was reading…"

A high-pitched wail escaped from Jenny's chest.

Shit. Were people hearing this? Were people watching this, thinking I made her cry? *Had* I made her cry? Shit. I should never speak. Or act. Ever. I screw everything up.

"You okay, Jen?" I asked. I subtly scooted a few inches away from her, with the caution of a man diffusing a bomb. What were you supposed to do with a crying girl? Would she want me to hug her? Give her a tissue? I didn't have a tissue! I suddenly wished I was in Indiana, during the days when I didn't even talk to girls.

Then I felt Jenny pull at my arm. She was dragging me over toward her. Surprised by her force, I stumbled across the sidewalk and suddenly found myself in a dark space between two buildings, all shadowed pavement and fire escapes. We were alone in an alley.

I turned my head rapidly from one side to another, from the piles of trash bags on one side to the squared-off view of the street on the other. I didn't want to look Jenny in the face.

"Turn me," she whispered.

Then I had to look, and frankly, she looked bat-shit crazy. Her tears were like magnifying glasses that made her crazy eyes seem bigger and scarier. My own eyes widened in response.

"What?"

I barely got the word out before she had me pinned against the alley wall. Her little palms were pressing into my jacket like she was making me into a kindergarten handprint project.

"Turn me," she repeated ominously, her little chin thrust toward me, her eyes looking like they could shoot lasers out of them.

For a wild second I thought, is Jenny going to take advantage of me? I was kind of okay with that. I was pretty sick of hauling my virginity around, and obviously Kate wasn't interested in taking it from me.

"Jenny, I…" I reached a nervous hand out for her arm, but her tendons tensed like rope. Was everyone in the world stronger than I was?

"Turn me into a vampire," she said.

A brief light from a window above blinded me in my shock.

"What?"

Her arms went slack and I could finally take a full breath.

"I want to be like you," she said, her voice shaking, her little hands trembling, her lips quivering.

"I want to be cool like you. I want everyone to talk about me. I want to be cool and not care what I say or what I do. Or who I hurt."

What? Who had I hurt?

"I'll be better than Kate," Jenny said earnestly, bringing her arms down to her sides, her face, hopeful, turned up at me. "I'll be a vampire, like you. I'll stay with you. She won't."

Something twisted in my chest. Jenny *liked* me. It hurt to have her stand there and tell me, to reveal something to me that would most likely lead to hurt feelings and embarrassment. I saw a lot of my pathetic self in her at that moment. No wonder Jenny had shut up as soon as I mentioned Kate. She was jealous. I was always patting myself on the back for being so perceptive, believing girls would like me because I was sensitive, aware of their feelings, but in the three months of having her constantly around, complaining to me, gossiping, copying my homework, I hadn't noticed that Jenny liked me. Even when Jenny went on and on about Kate's jeans, and Kate's sweating in gym class, and how Kate wouldn't understand me, I never even suspected the truth. Jenny liked me.

Jenny liked *me*. All my life, I'd waited for a girl to like me, or a middle-aged woman to like me, or a nun, or *anyone*. I'd thought a girl liking me would make me, to borrow a phrase from everyone who talks about my brother, "the man." Now Jenny liked me; apparently she'd liked me for a long time— and I'd never felt so terrible in my life. Even when Kate lied to me. Even when Celine rejected me.

"Finbar, please," Jenny begged.

Oh, shit, right. Back to this. Not only had I hurt Jenny, I'd also told her a massive lie. And this was karma coming back to kick my ass in a back alley. Sure, I'd noticed increasing numbers of girls discussing my vampire potential and debating my strength. And sure, Kayla Bateman had freaked out about me potentially drinking her blood. I knew they all believed, but… Jenny *really* believed. I didn't know it would go this far.

My palms got sweaty. I mean, I did owe Jenny. I'd been inconsiderate of her feelings. I'd treated her as badly as Celine had treated me. I owed her at least a metamorphosis. Problem was…

"Jenny, I don't know how," I told her.

Raising my hand to my indented chest, I surveyed the damage her fierce little palms had done when she pushed me. No broken ribs. Phew.

"You *do* know how."

"I don't." Against the alley wall, my shoulders rose in a hopeless shrug.

"You became one," she accused me, bitterly, from the throat.

Well, I was going to have to turn Jenny into a vampire. Of all the shitty situations I'd dug myself into lately, this one was pretty deep. How could I "turn" Jenny? My Catholic side told me there should be some kind of ceremony. Like the way I got ashes on Ash Wednesday, and how the priest put oil on my head at my confirmation. I looked around for what I could use. *With the contents of this herpes-rimmed Pepsi can, I anoint thee, Jenny, a vampire.* Or, *With the blood of this one-eyed pigeon, I anoint thee…* My options were pretty sketchy.

Luckily, Jenny was more specific.

"Bite me," she pleaded.

She made her neck extra naked for me, pulling down her collar, revealing a few freckles I'd never seen before.

Oh, Jesus. Lord's name in vain again, yes. But I really needed help here.

Against my will, without a plan, I felt my head tilt down toward her neck. There was quite a distance to bridge between my beanpole body and her elfin self, and the whole distance I was thinking, *What the hell am I gonna do?*

But then a thought occurred to me. It was like I suddenly had the wisdom of a thousand-year-old man. Or at least someone old enough to drink.

I made like I was going for her neck, the curve where it met her collarbone, and I did linger close for a few seconds, feeling the desperate heat emanating from those freckles. But then I took a detour. I went up to Jenny's ear instead, and I told her this:

"Turn yourself."

She pulled back like I had bad breath.

"What?"

"Turn yourself," I commanded her. "Just decide that you are someone else. Decide that you are a vampire. If you believe you're a vampire, everyone will believe you're a vampire."

"No." Jenny trembled. "No, they won't."

I leaned closer to her again.

"You believed me," I said.

I made a sudden move, snapping my teeth together, and Jenny trembled at the elbows.

"See," I said smoothly.

"What?" Jenny asked. "You're not really a vampire?"

"No!" I jumped in quickly. "I mean, yes. Well, kinda. I'm *mostly* a vampire. I have all the...aura, you know? The vampire aura. I have vampire attitude, too. I have the aura, and the attitude. I just don't, um, drink blood."

Jenny's small face was very serious. "So you're not *technically* a vampire?"

Well, technically...I called on Chauncey Castle's ability to answer a question with a question and coupled it with my extensive knowledge of Jenny.

"Would you want to *technically* be a vampire, Jenny?" I asked. "No more chai tea. No more onion bagels from Dunkin' Donuts. Plus...you know, you'd be dead. So you'd never get your driver's license."

We were already in a dark alley, but the idea of never getting her license was *really* scary to Jenny. Her arms dropped, freeing my chest and letting me inhale again. Her shoulders dropped, too.

"I guess I wouldn't want to *technically* be a vampire," she said. "I mean, I'd probably rather be Tresora Chest from *The Seductress and the Swashbuckler*. Or Raven Mane from *Dragons and Drama Queens*. She's the one I dyed my hair to look like," Jenny added, looking up at me.

"Ohhh." I tried to nod admiringly at her hair, which had grown out so far that it was two-thirds orange and only a third black.

"But no one even noticed when I dyed my hair." Jenny said, shaking her head. "None of the kids I've gone to school with for twelve years."

Oh, Jesus, I thought. I really needed to invest in some pocket tissues if I was gonna hang out with so many girls.

But Jenny wasn't crying when she looked up at me. And then she said something really thoughtful.

"I guess I didn't want to be a vampire," Jenny said. "I just wanted to be someone else."

Right after that, Jenny led the way out of the alley and down the street toward Grand Central and our train home. As I followed her little trudging footsteps, I should have felt bad for the girl. With her badly dyed hair and her too-big black jacket, she looked like she'd been kicked out of the Addams family. And suddenly I thought of all these things to comfort her, like some vague compliment Jason Burke had said that week, or the fact that the Irish author Gareth actually seemed semi-intrigued by Jenny, and he'd glanced at her a few times during his reading.

But what she'd said, she'd said so matter-of-factly, like it was normal. "I just wanted to be someone else." And, I guess, it was normal. Why else would I have given a sex speech in my English class and beat up a bully? Those weren't Finbaresque actions. Why else would I have become a vampire?

It seemed so simple now. Somehow quirky little Jenny had simplified it. She wanted to be someone else. I wanted to be someone else. And we couldn't be the only ones, either. I bet even Luke wanted to be someone else, sometimes — someone who could pass math or sit still through a test. And even Kate, Kate had wanted...

No. I was still angry about Kate. I couldn't think about her yet.

"Come on," Jenny called from ahead of me on the sidewalk. "We're just in time for the express train if you hurry up."

chapter

It took me a full week to notice that Luke was actually pretty depressed. Ever since the house party in New Rochelle, he had been so down that he didn't even throw things at the ceiling at night. He would just sigh, roll over, and go to sleep. While Luke habitually treated our stairwells and house siding like a playground, he only climbed through the second-story window once that week. And we legitimately needed his help to unlock the door.

"So how's, uh, Math B going?" I asked him one day when he was studying at my desk (his was, as usual, covered in sweaty clothes). Usually Luke wasn't really attentive when he was studying. I was impressed with his concentration today. He wasn't studying, but he had been doing a rubber-pencil trick for, like, fifteen minutes straight.

"Fine," he said, and shrugged.

I probed, pushed, and prodded sensitive points to find out why he was upset. This technique I've learned from my mother.

"Are you gonna fail?" I asked.

"Doubt it," Luke said. "I got a B on the last test."

"Luke! That's crazy good!"

"Yeah." And then he sighed again. What was this sigh? I'd never heard Luke sigh. Then a thought occurred to me. Luke was acting calmer.

"Did you go back on meds?" I asked him suddenly.

He turned around in my wooden desk chair and raised an eyebrow. Then he shook his head. "No."

Twin brothers are kind of like seesaws. When one of us goes down, the other automatically goes up. I don't mean that I was happy to see Luke upset. Rather, when I observed that he was upset, I became more upbeat in order to cheer him up. Or became more annoying in order to distract him.

"Hey," I called to him from my bed. "You got a little beard growing there?"

Was my brother really too depressed to shave? What was this?

I stood up and walked over to Luke. Indeed, he had kind of a beard. He had a quarter-inch of stubble.

"Ooh, sexy beard," I told him. "It's kind of ... red."

"I know," he said. "I don't know why."

Luke's hair was a lighter brown than mine. But his beard was kind of reddish-brown.

"You've got your Irish side showing," I told him. "Very nice. Can I touch it?"

"Nah," Luke said. "Don't touch it."

I reached out for his cheek. He slapped my hand away with those cheetah reflexes that have made so many high school football rivals cry. I reached again, quicker, and he missed.

"Ooh, sexy," I said, rubbing my brother's face.

See? I get pretty silly when Luke's not Luke. One of us has to be crazy at all times to justify my mother's paranoia.

"Sexy like a cactus."

"Yeah, yeah," Luke said. "Let me do this math stuff."

"C'mon, Luke," I said. "What's up with you?"

He turned this mournful, hound-dog-like face to me.

"All right, here it is," he said, lifting my desk chair. He turned the chair around and sat back down for the big reveal.

"I'm in love," Luke said.

I burst out laughing. "No, you're not. You're drugged up!"

"I'm in love," Luke repeated mournfully.

"You're pissed off because you're in love?" I asked him. "What are you, that little kid from *Love Actually*?"

Luke looked like himself for a minute.

"You really watch too many movies with Mom," he told me.

"Who's this girl?" I asked him. "Was she at the football party?"

Luke nodded.

"Was she the girl who was grinding so hard on you she got rug burn?" I asked.

"No," Luke said.

"Was she the one who took a tequila shot off your stomach?"

"No."

"Was she the one who took eight pictures with you and then cried because she dropped her digital camera?"

"No, not that one," Luke said. "I didn't actually talk to her at the party."

"Wait," I interrupted. "She wasn't busy arguing about Chris Brown songs, was she?"

"No," said Luke.

"Phew."

"She didn't stay long," Luke said. "She doesn't really like parties. And she doesn't like football, so I can't get to her that way."

"Well, what does she like?" I asked.

"Books," Luke said glumly. "Wait!"

Jumping up from the desk, Luke knocked my chair over. He had his energy back. I felt the need to issue a tornado warning for the tristate area.

"You can help me!" Luke said. He literally jumped up and down. Our floorboards creaked in protest.

"Finn, you can help me! This girl likes *books*! You must know her!"

"How would I know her?" I asked.

"Oh, come on," Luke said. "All you people who read know each other."

"People who read books?" I said. "No, we don't all know each other. But maybe I'll start a Facebook group."

"Finn, this is brilliant!" Luke was still pumped. "You can definitely help me out! She's your kind of girl. She's smart, she's quiet, she's terrible at kegstands...."

"One time," I groaned.

"But you can help me!"

I shook my head. "I have my own girl problems, Luke."

"You owe me," Luke told me. "Come on, help me out! I've helped you with girls before."

I scoffed. "You invited me to one party with Kate," I said. "I got punched, and she left."

"I've been helping you get girls all your life!" Luke wheedled.

"All my life?" I questioned. "Kate was my first girl!"

"Hey, what about..." Luke racked his brain. "Hey, what about, remember that librarian you liked when we were little?"

I feigned ignorance. "Librarian? I don't remember."

Luke rounded his hands out from his chest. The universal sign for "big boobs."

"All right," I admitted. "Yeah, what about her?"

"Remember that time you had a broken ankle and the fire alarm went off in the library and that librarian carried you out, all, like, wrapped in her arms?" Luke asked, with a surprisingly accurate memory. "She carried you out, man."

"Yeah," I admitted. I did remember. The librarian had picked me up and held me to her chest as we evacuated beneath the flashing fire alarm. I'd felt so safe and nonflammable between her breasts.

"So what's that got to do with you?" I asked.

"I knew you liked her," Luke said. "So I set that up."

"You pulled the alarm?" I asked, shocked.

"No!" Luke protested. Then he grinned. "I set the fire."

I laughed out loud, which I shouldn't have, because setting a fire in a place full of paper is a dumbass thing to do. But Luke did it, and it didn't end in disaster because he's protected by all the good luck I didn't inherit.

"Well, I guess I could tell you some things to read." I shrugged. "Do you know what kind of books this girl likes?"

"Um..." Luke looked away. I'd never seen him look embarrassed or awkward before. Oh, wow, finally—there was the family resemblance.

"She likes werewolf books," he mumbled sketchily.

"Wait, Luke," I began suspiciously. "You *hate* beards. They itch inside your football helmet. And there's no way you want people to know you're a redhead. You look like a leprechaun."

"Yeah, well..." Luke continued mumbling.

"I know what you're doing!" I crowed in triumph. "You're—"

"All right!" Luke said. "All right! I know! I'm kind of —"

"YOU'RE BECOMING A WEREWOLF!" I yelled. Then I cracked up in hysterical laughter.

"I'm not *becoming* a werewolf," Luke corrected me. For once, he cared about semantics. "I'm just...rocking a werewolf look. I mean, I'm not gonna *bite* anyone."

"You're so copying me!" I protested. "*I* became a vampire, and *I* didn't bite anyone!"

I knocked Luke on the shoulder, which was dumb, because he felt pretty much like a concrete wall.

"I'm not copying you!" Luke said. "A werewolf is totally different than a vampire! You're creepy all the time. Mine is just, like, a monthly thing...."

"Like PMS?" I suggested.

"Shut up!"

I laughed at Luke, and I walked away, saying, "Man. You've always wanted to be just like me."

That Sunday, I was supposed to go running with Jason Burke in preparation for our first winter track practice on Monday. It didn't happen. Jason had a hook-up-related injury. While he was getting with Kayla Bateman at a party that weekend, she climbed on top of him and he got crushed by her breasts. I'm serious. His doctor told him he cracked a rib.

"I may have told my mom that you elbowed me on the track," Jason added when he called me up to cancel our workout.

"What the hell, Jay?"

"Well, I couldn't tell her the truth," he said, which was fair.

Because Jason couldn't go running, I decided to ditch the workout altogether and go to the library. Actually, I've done this a few times. Whenever my personal trainer, Luke, assigns me a solo run, I tend to run as far as the end of our block, and then, when I'm out of his sight, walk to the library. Luke has no idea.

Today I walked up the steps to the redbrick library and greeted Agnes and one other librarian who knows me by name. Sadly, these were some of the few women left in my life, now that I was no longer anything with Kate.

Today was a poetry day, I decided. The poetry section was in the same mildewy corner where I'd been busted reading *Bloodthirsty*. The book I sat down with now was far less scandalous: *The Collected Poems of W. B. Yeats*. Yeats is this Irish poet who never got the girl, the girl being a hot Irish revolutionary named Maud Gonne. He wrote a ton of poems about her, but it never worked out between them. She liked more manly, non-poem-writing dudes. He couldn't be someone he wasn't. I sympathize.

Although to be honest, I was kind of relieved I wasn't a vampire anymore. It was annoying to come up with philosophical answers for things. It was a pain to avoid eating or drinking in public. And I hadn't successfully "glamoured" one person, not even Agnes when I tried to "glamour" her into excusing my late fees. I was thinking how relaxing it would be to stop my whole vampire thing, even contemplating taking class naps like Matt Katz, when I looked up and saw Kate walking toward me. She was wearing this too-big sweatshirt that went over her hands (my neurotic mind told me it was an ex-boyfriend's. Some guy she used to "do stuff with" back in the day. Shudder. Drop that thought). She came over to my table but stood a foot back from the chair opposite mine.

"Hi," Kate said. She spoke even softer than you were supposed to in the library.

"How'd you know I was here?" I asked immediately.

"I was tutoring Luke," Kate said. "He said you said you were out running, but you'd probably end up at the library."

I was so surprised I gave myself a paper cut and dripped a little blood on a self-loathing poem.

"What? But Luke didn't…"

"He knows you better than you think," Kate said.

"So why'd you come?" I asked.

"Well, among other reasons…"

Kate examined my face, but I didn't warm to her and I didn't smile. She continued, "I had to return something. A book."

A small leather book dropped out of the sleeve of Kate's sweatshirt. The gold-engraved letters were familiar to me. *The Sonnets of William Shakespeare.* I had told Kate about Shakespeare's sonnets at one of our lunches.

I looked at the book instead of Kate. I wasn't ready to forgive her. While I was looking down, she took the seat across from mine and opened the book.

"I think this one has some of my favorite lines," Kate said, slowly turning the pages. "Sonnet twenty-nine." Her lips pouted a little as she carefully pronounced the old-fashioned words:

> *When in disgrace with fortune and men's eyes,*
> *I all alone beweep my outcast state…*
> *And look upon myself, and curse my fate,*
> *Wishing me like to one more rich in hope,*
> *Featur'd like him, like him with friends possess'd…*
> *Yet in these thoughts myself almost despising,*
> *Haply I think on thee, — and then my state…*
> *For thy sweet love remember'd such wealth brings*
> *That then I scorn to change my state with kings.*

"I think I like it," Kate explained, "because it's about...not liking yourself. And wanting to change. Wanting to be popular and other stupid stuff that doesn't matter. Until you find someone who lets you be yourself. Which is even better than being a king...or, you know, a queen."

"Thanks for the analysis," I said. "But I've read it."

When I met Kate's eyes across the table, she leaned forward. She set the leather book of sonnets beside my book. Her hands in their balled-up sweatshirt-fists slid across the table so they were closer to my hands.

"I didn't lie to you, Finbar," Kate said. "I lied to everyone at my old school. I pretended to care about parties and kissing random guys. I don't. I kept that picture in my locker to remind me how much it sucked to care about all that stuff. I pretended with them. But I didn't pretend with you."

I lifted the leather-bound book from the table, flipped through its pages, but didn't read a word. I saw Kate's fists tighten in her sweatshirt, heard her holding her breath.

"What's this guy's name again?" I asked, flipping back to the title page of the book.

Kate looked confused for a minute, then she let out her breath and allowed herself to smile.

"Shakespeare?" I continued. "Hmmm, never heard of him."

"He never made it big," Kate teased, shaking her head. "Kind of an emo, underground guy."

"Ahhh." I nodded. When I saw Kate smiling across the table, I couldn't help but smile too. She got what I was hinting by reviving our lame Shakespeare joke.

"So you forgive me?" she asked.

"I guess it's only fair," I said, putting the Shakespeare book down again beside my Yeats. "I mean, I didn't always give you a totally...accurate picture of me, either."

"Oh, yeah?" Kate tilted her head against her sweatshirt hood. "I *knew* Finbar couldn't be your real name."

Rolling my eyes, I said, "God, I wish *that* were true."

"So who's the real Finbar?" Kate challenged as she sat down and rested her head on her hands to listen.

"Well, for one thing." I scratched my fingernail into the wooden table. "I'm allergic to the sun. I watch Kate Hudson movies with my mom. Every librarian in this building knows me by name. I'm scared of your dad's cooking, I'm intimidated as hell by you, and I am definitely not a vampire."

Kate laughed and reached her oversize sleeves across the two books to rest them on top of my hands, which were, of course, freakishly cold. She didn't ask about my sun condition; she didn't question my taste in movies; she didn't mock my librarian fetish. She just said, "I'll tell my dad to go with burgers on Friday."

"Friday?"

"We wanted to have you over again," Kate said. "My sisters and brother want to meet my boyfriend."

Jealousy and nausea surged through my stomach. I stuttered, but just before I spoke, I realized Kate was talking about me.

"Uh, boyfriend?" I repeated dumbly.

Although Kate shrugged like it didn't matter, I could see her fingers tense and curl around her sleeve.

"If you want," she said.

And I said, "Cool."

It was that simple. Kate's sweatshirt may have been someone else's, but Kate was mine. We left both books on the table and I gave Agnes the librarian a wink as Kate and I walked out together. I wasn't the stud my mother's notes had predicted, I wasn't the vampire heartthrob Ashley and Kayla had hoped for, and I wasn't the muscled Finbar 2.0 that Luke's training regimen had aimed for. I was just the guy driving Kate home. But that's exactly who I wanted to be.

"By the way," I told Kate as I opened my passenger door for her, "Luke's a werewolf now."

"What?" she asked.

"He's pretending to be a werewolf to impress a girl." I shook my head. "Sorry bastard."

"I've got to say, though," Kate said critically, "I could never believe you as a vampire. But I could really see Luke as a werewolf."

"Oh, yeah?" I bared my teeth menacingly at her. "Wait till I turn you."

Kate laughed.

"Don't tell your mother about Luke being a werewolf," she said. "I have a feeling she'd freak out about fur on the furniture."

acknowledgments

Many thanks to the following people:

My agent, Daniel Lazar, for guiding me through the publication of my first book, and somehow making every step of the process easy and pleasant.

My editor, Elizabeth Bewley, for her thoughtful suggestions and advice, and everyone at Little, Brown who fell in love with Finbar Frame.

My family and friends, especially Lucila Farina, who inspired me with her love of vampire pop culture, and Christine Becker, who thought *Bloodthirsty* was hilarious before she read even a word of it.